Luke Sutton: Mustanger

Luke Sutton: Mustanger

LEO P. KELLEY

A DOUBLE D WESTERN
DOUBLEDAY
NEW YORK   LONDON   TORONTO   SYDNEY   AUCKLAND

A DOUBLE D WESTERN
PUBLISHED BY DOUBLEDAY
a division of Bantam Doubleday Dell Publishing Group, Inc.
666 Fifth Avenue, New York, New York 10103

DOUBLE D, DOUBLEDAY, and the portrayal of the letters DD are trademarks of Doubleday, a division of Bantam Doubleday Dell Publishing Group, Inc.

Library of Congress Cataloging-in-Publication Data

Kelley, Leo P.
    Luke Sutton: mustanger / Leo P. Kelley.
       p.   cm.—(Double D western)
    I. Title.
PS3561.E388L838   1990   89-37606
813'.54—dc20   CIP
ISBN 0-385-24186-0

Luke Sutton: Mustanger

ONE

SITTING ON THE EDGE OF THE BED in his room in Nevada's International Hotel, Virginia City, Luke Sutton spat on the black high-topped townsman's shoe that was fitted over his left hand like a stiff leather glove. Then he began to buff it vigorously with the brush he held in his other hand. When it gleamed to his satisfaction, he repeated the process with the other shoe.

After putting both shoes on, he pulled on his beige trousers and bent down to fasten their cloth straps under the insteps of his shoes. While whistling "Oh, Promise Me," he put on a white tucked linen shirt and then an elaborately embroidered brown satin waistcoat. After rejecting a neckcloth, he chose instead a white silk cravat which he fastened around his neck. Then he put on his brown frock coat and stepped back to take a good look at himself in the mirror that hung on the wall above the marble-topped dresser.

The man he saw staring back at him was tall, leanly built, and tautly muscled. He hadn't an extra ounce of flesh anywhere on his body. His shoulders were broad, his hips narrow. His eyes were the color of woodsmoke and in them was a look of keen alertness.

His hair was straight and black and long enough to bury both his ears and the nape of his neck. He had a thin nose and lips that were also thin, above a square jaw. His face was flat-planed in places, sharply angled in others. It was a face that more than one woman had found handsome and more than one man had found threatening.

Well, now, he said silently to himself as he continued to study his reflection in the mirror. Don't you look the dandy? You sure are one dolled-up dude, there's no two ways around that.

He carefully adjusted his cravat until it looked exactly the way he wanted it to. Then, picking up the envelope that lay on top of the dresser, he opened it and took out an engraved invitation, which he proceeded to read for the third or fourth time.

It informed him that Mr. and Mrs. Ronald Wilson were pleased to announce the marriage of their daughter, Violet, to Mr. Aaron Endicott. Flowery phrases requested the pleasure of Mr. Lucas Sutton's company at the ceremony—scheduled to take place this very day—and at the reception which would follow in the basement of the church.

He returned the invitation to the dresser, took from a wall peg his brown felt hat, which was cut in the "gentleman's style," and placed it on his head at a slightly rakish angle.

He left the room still whistling "Oh, Promise Me," and boarded the hotel's hydraulic elevator.

When he emerged into the lobby below, he headed for the door that led to the street, not missing the openly admiring look a young woman gave him as he passed by.

Once outside, he strode briskly down C Street. It was not long before he reached the church, from which wafted strains of the song he had been whistling earlier. Men and women streamed into the church, attired, like Sutton himself, in finery—the men in morning coats and some of them top hats, the women in rainbow-hued dresses, all of them.

He joined the throng entering the church, and once inside found himself a seat in a pew midway between the door and the altar. He did not have long to wait. Within minutes of his arrival, the organist's "Oh, Promise Me" gave way to the stately strains of *Lohengrin's* wedding march. Like everyone else, Sutton, his hat in his hand, rose and turned toward the rear of the church.

And there she was—Violet Wilson, a young woman of striking beauty who was wearing a floor-length wedding dress of robin's egg blue, trimmed with ostrich tips, lace, and braid. Behind her, two little girls in matching organdy dresses carried her train.

To the continued strains of the wedding march, she made her way down the aisle toward the altar carrying a bouquet of lilies of the valley, a single red rose tucked in among them.

When she reached the altar, Sutton watched with the rest of the congregation as an elegantly attired Aaron Endicott joined her in front of the minister, who held a small leather-bound book in his pale hands.

The organ fell silent.

The minister cleared his throat and intoned the familiar words: "Dearly beloved, we are gathered together here today . . ."

Sutton, as he listened to the other, also familiar, words about promising to love and honor—for Aaron Endicott—and promising to love, honor, and obey—for Violet Wilson—found himself drifting back in his mind to another time and place—and another woman.

The place was Texas, the time over four long years ago. The woman—Elizabeth Dacey. He could see her lovely face now in his mind's eye, almost feel the touch of her skin against his, hear the soft lilt of her voice as she called him "darling" and talked of the life they would share when they were married . . .

"Will you take this woman . . ."

The minister's words became a part of Sutton's reverie, as did Aaron Endicott's firm "I will."

With his eyes wide open, Sutton continued dreaming of Elizabeth Dacey and his lost love for her—the love they had shared as they had planned to spend their lives together; then bullets had put an ugly end to their dream and launched Sutton on a years-long hunt for the four men who had taken part in the brutal and cold-blooded murder of his younger brother, Dan.

He left Elizabeth behind on the day he had set out after the killers. Throughout the years that followed he was consumed—obsessed—by the hunt. It became his life, and his life became one that was stripped bare of all else, including love.

When his hunt finally ended successfully, he had thought he would be able to resume his former life at his homeplace in Texas—and marry Elizabeth Dacey. It was not to be. His telegraph message telling her that he would soon return to the homeplace and to her loving arms brought a reply from her that stunned him. Elizabeth, in his absence, had married and become the mother of a ten-month-old daughter.

Her answering telegraph message, which told him how the world had changed so radically when he wasn't looking, made him feel bereft. And then angry. Angry at himself for having been a fool, one who had lost touch with the woman he loved for so long and had still expected her to be patiently waiting upon his pleasure. But no, he had told himself at the time, it wasn't like that at all. She should have understood. She should have—what? Waited four long years—and maybe even more—to hear from a man obsessed with a lust for vengeance that took him throughout the world of the West, one who never wrote, one who might, as far as Elizabeth Dacey knew, be dead and buried?

Looking then at her message in his hand, he knew there was no going back. Knew that the four men who had murdered his brother had also murdered his hopes and plans for the future. He had gained the vengeance he had so eagerly sought. But he had lost his beloved Elizabeth.

"Will you, Violet, take this man . . ."

Sutton's eyes focused on the couple standing in front of the minister, and he envied them the life together that they were beginning this day. In them, he saw embodied a dream that had once been his and Elizabeth's.

"The ring."

He watched as Endicott took a plain gold ring from his pocket and placed it on Elizabeth's—no, he corrected himself, on Violet's—finger.

"—pronounce you husband and wife."

He watched Endicott bend and kiss his new bride's uplifted lips. He continued watching as the new Mrs. Aaron Endicott walked with her husband, to the organist's renewed music, back down the aisle and out into the morning's bright sunlight.

Then he, together with the rest of the people in the church, followed the couple outside where well-wishes were shouted and a white rain of rice drowned the bride and groom.

Women rushed up to kiss the cheeks of both the bride and groom. Men shook Endicott's hand.

Sutton, too, went up and shook the groom's hand. "Congratulations, Aaron," he said. "A long and happy life to the both of you."

"Luke, it's good to see you," Endicott said, pumping Sutton's hand. "We were afraid you might not be able to come."

"Neither flood nor fire could have kept me away from this happy occasion," Sutton assured him.

"Oh, Luke, it's you!" Violet cried as she caught sight of Sutton and freed herself from the enveloping embrace of a plump woman in a noisy taffeta dress. She threw her arms around his neck and pressed her cheek to his.

He embraced her, placed a chaste kiss on her cheek, and whispered, "May all your troubles be little ones, Violet."

"You're coming to the wedding breakfast, aren't you?" she asked.

"Wouldn't miss it for the world and all its wonders."

"I am truly a blessed woman, aren't I?" Violet asked, "considering the fact that I have two of the dearest men in the world at my side on this the happiest day of my life!"

Taking her husband's and Sutton's arms, she led both men to the entrance to the church basement where the wedding breakfast was to be held.

Once down the stairs and in the great hall that held tables topped with linen tablecloths and vases filled with black-eyed Susans, Sutton began to scan the tables for the place card bearing his name.

Violet, her arm still linked in his as she responded to the many well-wishers who crowded around her, did not at first notice what he was doing. But when she did, she tightened her grip on his arm and said, "You sit with us at the head table, Luke. Excuse us for now, won't you?"

Sutton headed for the table Violet had indicated, and she and her husband joined the receiving line.

Some time later, they rejoined Sutton who told them, "Putting me here in a place of honor like you two've done kind of takes me by surprise, to tell you the truth. I was expecting something much more modest. Though everything in this room looks real pert and pretty and not the least bit modest."

"As well it should," Endicott declared. "This is a once-in-a-lifetime day for us, Luke. We both wanted it to be as special as we could possibly make it."

Sutton nodded, with a wave of his hand that encompassed the tables, the strategically placed candelabras and wall sconces with their lighted candles, and the colorful crepe-paper streamers strung across the ceiling in looping strands.

A door on one side of the room opened to admit a cloud of steam, and several women entered carrying silver tureens.

The women moved among the tables, spooning out soup from the tureens. Soon, in addition to the low hum of conversation, the sound of silverware against china plates could also be heard, as the wedding guests began the first course of what would prove to be a sumptuous wedding breakfast.

The serving women and their tureens vanished through the steam that was still drifting into the room. When they reappeared, they proceeded to serve boiled ham studded with cloves, crisp roast turkey, oysters, a bean salad and a garden salad, warm bread and muffins, butter, bride's cake, fruit cake, jelly cake, coffee, tea, and champagne.

When one of the serving women had filled Violet's, Endicott's, and then Sutton's glasses with champagne, Sutton raised his glass. "To the happy couple," he toasted.

They touched glasses and drank, after which Endicott said, "I too have a toast to offer." With Violet looking at him expectantly, he said, "To you, Luke. Without your help, this day might never have been."

Violet smiled and, turning to Sutton, raised her glass. "I can't tell you how much and how sincerely I share Aaron's feelings, Luke."

They touched glasses again and drank.

A three-piece band consisting of fiddle, piano, and guitar began to play. It continued playing for the next hour, during which the wedding guests made short and happy work of the mountains of food that had been placed before them.

Then the tables were cleared, except for coolers of champagne and pots of coffee and tea, and moved back so the dancing could begin. It was led by Violet and Endicott who were given the floor all to themselves at first, before they were joined by many of their guests.

At the end of the first dance, Sutton saw Violet whisper something to her husband and then watched as Endicott crossed the room toward him.

"Luke," Endicott said when he reached Sutton, "Violet wonders would you do her the honor of dancing the next dance with her."

"It would be my honor, Aaron. Sutton immediately joined Violet. As the band struck up a waltz, he took the bride in his arms and they began to dance. They were silent at first but then Violet drew away from him and, looking up into his eyes, said, "I bless the day I came to you and hired you to find Aaron for me. I sometimes shudder to think what might have happened if I had not done so. Dade Talbot might well have . . ."

When she left her sentence unfinished, Sutton said, "I'm just glad I was able to find him for you and see to it that you two got back together where you belonged. Now it seems you're both bound together for sure."

"Till death do us part," Violet quoted in a gay voice that belied the solemnity of her words, as she spun gracefully in Sutton's arms and music flooded the room. Then, looking mischievously up at him again, she said, "I have told everyone I know—and even some strangers as well—about how you searched for Aaron and how you finally found him and then how you saved both of our lives and—"

"Hold on there," Sutton said, laughing. "You'll run out of breath."

"Seriously, Luke, I am ever so grateful to you. It's because of you that I am so happy today and can look forward to a life filled with still more happiness in all the years to come."

When he started to protest, she put a finger on his lips, silencing him. They continued dancing but then, when he felt someone tap him on the shoulder, he responded by surrendering Violet to the smiling silver-haired man who had just cut in.

As the pair danced, Violet said something to her elderly partner and he turned to glance in Sutton's direction. Then, when the music ended moments later, she and her partner made their way over to where Sutton was standing.

"Luke," Violet said, "I hope you don't mind that my father cut in."

"Not at all. Pleased to make your acquaintance, Mr. Wilson."

"I've heard a lot about you, Mr. Sutton," Wilson said as the two men shook hands. "My daughter could talk of nothing else after you located Aaron for her and kept her from coming to harm at the hands of— what was that man's name, my dear?"

"Dade Talbot," Violet answered.

"A villain if there ever was one," Wilson exclaimed. "I'm forever in your debt, Mr. Sutton, for protecting my daughter from Talbot and for reuniting her with her beloved."

At that moment, Endicott joined them and swept his bride away with him as the music resumed.

"Come over to my table, if you will, Mr. Sutton," Wilson said, taking Sutton by the elbow and ushering him through the maze of tables. "I have something I would like to discuss with you."

When they reached the table where a lone woman sat, Wilson introduced her to Sutton as his wife.

"I am pleased to meet you, Mr. Sutton," said Mrs. Wilson as both men sat down at the table. "My daughter has told us about how you helped her despite grave danger to yourself. My husband and I are most grateful to you."

"I was glad I could be of help," Sutton said. "Glad too to see how things have turned out for her and Aaron."

Both parents turned doting eyes on their daughter and her husband as the pair danced together some distance away.

Wilson turned back to Sutton. "On our way out here, we passed through eastern Nevada. We made an overnight stop there. Early the next morning, long before the stagecoach left, I was out walking when I happened to see a sight that will stay with me for the rest of my life, I am certain."

Wilson paused, a faraway look in his eyes. Then, as if coming to himself again, he continued, "I saw a stallion that was without a doubt the most beautiful horse I have ever seen. He was standing on a ridge off to the west with the rising sun highlighting him. What a magnificent creature he was! He was like a golden statue of a horse—but not just any horse, oh, my, no! He was the very embodiment of all that is fine and noble about the species. He was not quite a sorrel color nor could he be described as a buckskin. His hide, as I've said, was more a golden color as were his mane and tail. At first, I thought it might be merely the sunlight that gave him such an unusual hue but I soon realized that such was not the case.

"As I continued watching him, totally awestruck, Mr. Sutton, the stallion made his way down from the ridge. I lost sight of him for several minutes and had almost begun to think that I had imagined seeing such a marvelous animal when a herd of mares and foals suddenly appeared. They were climbing a ridge opposite to the one where I had seen the stallion. Then, lo and behold, the stallion himself appeared behind the herd as he drove them up the mountainside."

Sutton was wondering what Wilson's account of his sighting a mustang, a magnificent one or not, had to do with him when Wilson continued, "Our daughter has told us a great deal about you, Mr. Sutton. Violet mentioned that you have been hired from time to time by a number of people to find missing persons for them."

"Yes, sir, that's true enough."

"Violet told us you have found every single person you went out to find. Is that also true?"

"It is."

"Do you know anything about horses, Mr. Sutton?"

Wilson's question took Sutton by surprise. "I know horses as well as the next man, I reckon. Matter of fact, four or so years ago I made my living down in Texas, where I had a homeplace at the time, as a mustanger—trapping, breaking, and selling wild horses."

Wilson's eyes seemed to light up. He turned excitedly to his wife, reached out, clasped her hands in his, and exclaimed, "This is really too good to be true, isn't it, my dear?"

Mrs. Wilson nodded and then both she and her husband turned their attention back to Sutton, who was still wondering where the conversation was leading.

Wilson said, "Mr. Sutton, I want to hire you to find the stallion I just told you about. I want you to break him and bring him back here to me."

Before Sutton could respond to Wilson's unexpected and somewhat startling request, Mrs. Wilson said, "My husband has neglected to tell you that we have a horse farm back in New Jersey, Mr. Sutton. Ronald runs a very fine and highly successful breeding program there. He is, I shall tell you quite truthfully, if immodestly, the most renowned breeder of horses east of the Mississippi River."

"I take it then, Mr. Wilson," Sutton said, "that you want to use this mustang you spotted in your breeding program."

"Yes, I do. But I also have other plans for him as well. I also intend to train him to become a race horse."

"My husband," Mrs. Wilson said with a small smile, "also owns and operates a racetrack in New Jersey, Mr. Sutton."

"You, Mr. Sutton," Wilson said with enthusiasm, "are the perfect man to go out after Wildfire. That, by the way, is the name the stallion is known by—or so I was told by our stage driver when I mentioned my sighting to him. You know horses, have even worked with them as a mustanger, as you just mentioned, and you're not only a man not to be deterred from any goal you set for yourself, according to our daughter, but also a man who is both brave and fearless in the pursuit of his goals."

"The fee, Ronald," Mrs. Wilson prompted.

"Ah, yes, your fee, Mr. Sutton. How much would you charge for such a venture?"

"I don't think—"

"One thousand dollars for the finding of Wildfire," Wilson interrupted, holding up one finger. "Another thousand dollars for breaking and delivering him here to me." Up went a second finger.

"That's a very generous offer, Mr. Wilson," Sutton said.

Wilson smiled broadly. "Then you'll do it?"

"I'd been about to say that I don't think I'm the right man for the job you've got in mind."

"Not the right man for the job?" Wilson spluttered. "You said you were a mustanger at one time. Violet said you were a bold and resourceful fellow. Of course you're the man for the job."

"Mr. Wilson, I've been in the business of hunting people, not horses."

"I'm fully aware of that," Wilson declared impatiently. "But it does seem to me, based on what you did for my daughter and the daring way you went about doing it, that the same skills you used in her case would be precisely the ones you would use in this one."

"I reckon that's so to one degree or another," Sutton admitted, "though I never thought of the matter quite in that way—never had to since nobody ever asked me to go run down some wild horse before."

"I'm asking you to do that now, Mr. Sutton."

"We would appreciate it if you would oblige us, Mr. Sutton," Mrs. Wilson interjected somewhat shyly, with a covert glance at her husband. "It means so much to us."

Sutton was reasonably sure that what Mrs. Wilson really meant was that it meant so much to Ronald Wilson. He strongly doubted that it mattered to her except insofar as it mattered to her husband.

"Do you have some other offer that you're letting override mine?" Wilson asked Sutton.

"It's not that."

"Then what is it?"

"Well, like I said before, it's a little out of my line."

"Nonsense!" Wilson exploded. "You're definitely the man for the job. I said it before and I'll say it again."

"Please, dear," Mrs. Wilson admonished gently, placing a hand on her husband's arm. "Mr. Sutton must make up his own mind."

Wilson absently patted his wife's hand, his eyes fixed on Sutton who continued, "I've read some stories about Nevada's wild horse herds. Our local newspaper has been running a whole series of them and from what I've read it seems to me that everybody and his Aunt Mary hates the herds. Cattlemen claim they ruin the range. Horse breeders complain about how the stallions like this Wildfire you spotted lure away their domesticated mares." Sutton paused. "I always thought it would be best if everybody just sort of took the attitude of live and let live. The wild horses, they've got a right to be in this world just the same as the rest of us."

Wilson's eyes narrowed. He lit a cigar and, jabbing its glowing end at Sutton, said, "That's odd talk coming from a man who has been a mustanger, I really must say."

"I know it is," Sutton agreed. "But since I was a mustanger things have happened to me—things that have changed me some. There once was a time when I lost my freedom, for example . . ."

As Sutton's voice trailed away, Wilson blew smoke into the air and said, "Violet mentioned something about you having been accused of a murder you didn't commit, and jailed for it."

Sutton nodded.

"Damn shame what happened to you," Wilson muttered. "Excuse me, my dear." Again he patted his wife's hand. "But I fail to see what—"

"Mr. Wilson," Sutton interrupted, "I was always a man you might call kind of fiddle-footed. I liked—still do like—to be as free as the breeze. Free to come and go when the fancy strikes me, which is exactly the way I lived—without crossing over the line into what some folks might call irresponsibility. But after I'd had me a taste of being locked up in that Texas jail, well, I came to value my freedom more than ever—almost as much as I valued my life.

"Hold on, Mr. Wilson. Don't say anything just yet. What I'm getting at is this. I don't anymore much relish the idea of trapping mustangs and breaking them. To me now it seems like—like—" Sutton, momentarily at a loss for words, hesitated. Then, "It's kind of like putting a bird in a cage. Some birds, when you do that to them, they forget how to sing. Or maybe it's not so much that they forget. Maybe it's that when you cage a free critter like a bird they just don't have the heart to sing anymore. It's like they're mourning the life they've lost. Their freedom. Same thing with a mustang. I've known them to—some of them—even after being green broke—to never let a man get on their

backs without they do a bunch of bucking and such.
One of them I broke and later sold—a stallion—he
committed suicide by throwing himself over a cliff.
The man I sold him to told me later he was riding the
stud one day when the horse all of a sudden—this was
just days after I'd sold him—took a notion to head
straight for the edge of a cliff. The man told me he
went for it without once so much as swerving an inch.
His head and neck, they were jutting out and nothing
the man riding him could do with the reins or the
bridle would slow down, let alone stop, that stud. He
wouldn't turn, even when the man jerked as hard as he
could on the reins and seesawed the bridle bit till he
had cut the horse's mouth almost to ribbons. When
that stallion put on one last big burst of speed, the man
told me, he knew the horse was a goner and he'd be
one too if he didn't do something and do it fast. He
threw himself out of the saddle and it was but seconds
later, as he lay there on the ground where he'd landed,
that he saw the horse go leaping off the cliff. He said
the horse was there one minute silhouetted against the
blue sky and then he was gone. He heard an awful
popping sound. He got up and went over to the edge
of the cliff and there was the busted body of his mount
three hundred yards down below. He always claimed,
and I for one believe him, that his horse just up and
decided to kill himself since he couldn't be free anymore."

"Forgive me for saying so, Mr. Sutton," Wilson remarked, "but that's hard to believe. A horse commit-
ting suicide? Really now."

"It's the truth, Mr. Wilson. The man who told me
that story—I'd known him for years and always found
him to be as honest as the day is long. But I can tell

you another story about something similar that happened to me personally.

"One time I took two mares I'd gentled along with me when I went out hunting a stud I had my heart set on trapping. Well, sir, after a spell of trailing him, trap that stud I finally did. I necked him like I'd planned on doing—"

" 'Necked him,' Mr. Sutton?" Mrs. Wilson asked, obviously puzzled by the term.

"Sorry, ma'am. I should have explained what I meant. 'Necking' a wild horse means looping a rope around his neck and then tying the two loose ends of the rope to the necks of the two other already broke horses which, like I said, I did to that stud using my two mares.

"He fought me every inch of every mile after I'd necked him. My mares trotted along as pretty as you please, but not him. He'd dig in his heels and try to hold back. The mares, they'd keep pulling on the rope around their necks and between the pair of them they came close to choking him to death. You could see his muscles straining as he fought that rope. When I reckon the pain he was feeling got so bad, he'd give in —but just for a little while. He'd spurt forward to put some slack in the rope and give himself a chance to catch his breath, and then he'd start the same thing all over again. It went on like that with neither him nor me giving in for a whole lot of miles. It soon became clear to me that that stallion was just not about to let me try to break him. It wasn't that he was a dumbbell either. He knew—I swear he did—exactly what he was doing. He just wouldn't give in to being caught. That horse was a fighter. He figured, the way I saw it at the time and still do, that he'd either break loose or die in the attempt, and die is what he wound up doing. He finally fell down dead between my two mares."

"I had no idea that such things could happen," a shocked Mrs. Wilson murmured. "Did you, Ronald?"

Her husband shook his head. "But—"

"You wouldn't want something as terrible as that to happen to Wildfire, would you, Ronald?" Mrs. Wilson inquired.

"No, of course, I wouldn't. But—"

"Neither would I," Sutton said, and got to his feet. "It was a real pleasure meeting you, ma'am. You too, Mr. Wilson," he added as he shook hands with the horse breeder. "I'm sorry I couldn't oblige you. I'm sure in time you'll find somebody else who can do the job you want done. There are a lot of mustangers around who'd jump at the chance to work for you under the generous terms you're offering."

Sutton bowed to Mrs. Wilson and then left the table and made his way across the room to where Violet and Endicott were still dancing together. He waited until the music ended and they were leaving the floor before approaching them.

"I'll be going now," he told them. "But I didn't want to leave without wishing you two the very best of everything this old world of ours has to offer to such special folks as yourselves."

"Thank you, Luke," Endicott said.

"Thank you too for coming to our wedding, Luke," Violet said.

"I wouldn't have missed it for all the tea in China and that's the truth. But now I think a little walking is in order, to clear my head after that sumptuous feast you provided this morning and I'm afraid I overindulged in. I feel as stuffed as a Christmas goose."

"You must be sure to come and visit us when we

return from our honeymoon and have set up house-keeping," Violet said warmly.

Sutton shook hands with Endicott, gave the smiling Violet an embrace, and then left as the couple made their way hand in hand back to the dance floor.

TWO

EARLY THE FOLLOWING MORNING, as Sutton was getting ready to leave his hotel room, there was a knock on the door. It took him by surprise because he was not expecting anyone, certainly not at such an early morning hour. He went to the door and opened it to find Violet Endicott standing in the hall.

"Well, I must say this is a surprise," he greeted her. "I thought you and Aaron would be well on your way to your honeymoon by now."

"We plan to leave later today," Violet said. "May I come in?"

"Sure you can." Sutton stepped aside and, after Violet had entered the room, closed the door. "Have a seat."

Violet sat down on a chair by the window and, when Sutton had seated himself on the edge of his unmade bed, she said, "I want to begin by apologizing to you for calling at such an unsuitable time, Luke."

"The hour don't matter, Violet. I'm always glad to see you. What's on your mind?"

"Father told me that you and he had a talk at the reception yesterday."

"That's right, we did. Nice man, your father. Your mother, she struck me as just as nice."

"He told me that he had asked you to try to trap Wildfire for him."

"Yep. He did."

"He also told me you turned him down and why you did. I told him that I thought your reasons for doing so made a great deal of sense. But despite that fact, I came here this morning, Luke, to ask you to reconsider Father's request. Wait! Before you say anything, please hear me out.

"I want you to know that Father is a man who has spent most of his life working with horses—breeding them, training them, buying and selling them, racing them. I have never in my life seen him mistreat a horse. I have seen him fire one of his grooms whom he once found whipping a horse in a fit of uncontrolled anger."

"Violet, you just said you understood my reasons for not wanting to try trapping Wildfire for your father. Well, I'm here to tell you that those reasons of mine haven't changed one whit. I haven't changed my mind about the matter."

"Father has his heart set on making Wildfire an integral part of his racing stable and breeding program," Violet continued as if she had not heard a word Sutton had just said. "He is convinced you are the man to find the stallion and to break it for him as he requested. So am I, after what I have seen you do on my behalf. Luke, you're courageous, strong—oh, there's no need for me to go into your many qualifications for the job."

"There are other mustangers," Sutton said, "who'd be more than happy to take on the job your father wants done. Why, he could hire more than one such man with the money he's willing to pay."

"I'm sure that's true, Luke. But Father doesn't want anyone else. He wants you because of what I told him about the bravery and determination you displayed when you helped Aaron and me. Now that he knows you also have experience as a mustanger, he is more than ever convinced that you're the man for the job. Won't you reconsider his offer, Luke?"

"I'd like to oblige your father, Violet. But I just can't see my way clear to do so. I'm dead set against seeing that stallion your father wants so bad broke and fenced in for the rest of his natural life."

"Would you rather see Wildfire dead?"

"I don't think I follow you."

Violet reached into her reticule and removed a copy of *The Territorial Enterprise.* "Father told me that you told him you had been reading the series of articles about Nevada's wild horse herds that have been running in the *Enterprise.* As a subscriber, so have I. This is the most recent edition of the paper. Have you seen it?"

Sutton shook his head.

"Please read the article on page three."

Sutton took the newspaper from Violet, opened it, and began to read the article that was headlined: "Wild Horses Doomed?"

The state legislature has just passed a bill endorsing the slaughter of the wild horse herds roaming throughout Nevada, particularly in the northern and eastern sections of the state. The bill authorizes the army to dispatch troops to the areas in question for the specific purpose of killing as many of the feral horses as possible.

A spokesman for the army, Captain Ralph Carrington, who is involved in the current extermination plan, is quoted as saying that he has been given orders to let the men in his command use the wild horses for target practice.

It is widely known that many voices have been raised against the presence of wild horse herds in

Nevada. Ranchers claim that the herds ruin the range and make it unfit for cattle. These ranchers, the perennial archenemy of the mustangs, also claim that the horses harass their stock, trample water holes, break water troughs, and, worst of all, eat the grass these men require for their cattle.

In opposition to the position taken by the ranchers are others who point out that when horse prices fall, as they inevitably and periodically do, these same cattlemen who profess such ire over the presence of the feral horses on the range turn out many of their own domesticated horses and seldom bother to reclaim them, thus adding to the problem of the rapidly growing horse herds against which they have railed so vocally and, it would now appear, so successfully.

A particular target of this legislative attack upon the feral horses is said to be a large band of mares and their foals controlled by a legendary, indeed almost mythic, stallion known locally as Wildfire. It is reliably reported that this stud is extremely intelligent, wily, and elusive. Men who have tried to trap him, and many have, have all failed to do so. One noted mustanger, Mr. Edward Harding, is reported to have said, referring to Wildfire, "There's not a man been born yet with enough sand, not to mention horse sense, that can catch that broomtail. The only way he can be caught is if he someday decides he wants to be."

It is rumored that, in addition to the legislation decreeing the legitimate slaughter of the horse herds, some ranchers are not relying on the law or the army to do the job. These men are said to have hired "stud killers." These are men who are assigned the task of shooting as many wild horses found on their employers' range as possible, for a specified per-head bounty to be paid by their employers.

It would thus appear that the days of the feral horses are numbered. It would also appear that the wily Wildfire, who has for years eluded the traps set for him by countless men with "mustang fever," may now not be able to escape the bullets of the target-practicing soldiers or those of the hired stud killers.

Sutton lowered the paper. His eyes met Violet's. Neither of them spoke for a long moment until Violet finally said, "They will kill him, Luke."

Sutton said nothing; a muscle in his jaw jumped.

"They will kill him," Violet repeated, "unless you can save him."

"Save him?"

"By trapping him and bringing him back here to my father before a soldier or a stud killer can shoot him."

Sutton looked down at the article he had just read.

"May I have that?"

"Beg pardon?" Sutton looked up at Violet, who was holding out her hand.

"The newspaper," she said.

He handed it to her. "I realize," she said softly, "that it may be an impossible task to trap Wildfire. It says here: 'Men who have tried to trap him, and many have, have all failed to do so.' It also says, or rather Mr. Harding, who is quoted in the article, says, 'There's not a man been born yet with enough sand, not to mention horse sense, that can catch that broomtail.' "

"Harding, whoever he is, doesn't know what he's talking about," Sutton said. "Any man who knows horses—a man who's got the guts to just keep at it could trap that stud using a parada or a corral, or he could do it at the animal's water hole which he could stake out—there are a whole lot of ways a man could do it if he went and put his mind to work on the problem."

"But the paper says Wildfire has outwitted numerous mustangers, Luke."

"He wouldn't outwit me. You can bet your bottom dollar on that."

"Well, I suppose I will have to take your word for that, won't I? I mean I'm not likely to see any proof of your claim, am I?"

Sutton, who had been staring thoughtfully out the window, suddenly turned to face Violet.

She met his gaze with an impassive expression.

"You sure do know how to work your way around a man and get him to do what you want him to do, don't you?" Sutton asked.

A faint smile appeared on Violet's face. "When I saw the article in the paper this morning, I was sure I could use it to make you change your mind about Father's offer. I was convinced that you wouldn't want to see a magnificent animal like Wildfire ruthlessly destroyed any more than Father would. You see, I know, Luke, that you are a proud man. I also know, and this is probably a more important element in the present situation, that you are the kind of man who would never—could not—walk away from a challenge. I felt certain that the quoted Mr. Harding's words about no one being able to catch Wildfire would be a challenge to your abilities as a former mustanger. And I was right, wasn't I? You have changed your mind, haven't you? You will try to trap Wildfire for Father?"

Sutton, bemused and beginning to grin, said,

"You're right. I have changed my mind. I'll go and try to catch that horse for your father."

Violet jumped up from her chair and, as Sutton also rose, she threw her arms around his neck, hugged him, and cried, "Father will be ever so pleased, Luke. And *I* am so pleased." Stepping back and suddenly sobering, she looked up at Sutton. "Do you think you can trap Wildfire before the soldiers and the stud killers can kill him?"

"Don't know, to tell you the truth. What I do know is I'm going to do my best to trap him and get him away from where he is before anybody can use him for target practice or to earn a bounty on his hide. Now, to move on to another matter. I haven't had breakfast. Have you?"

"No. I came here as soon as I read the article in the paper this morning without bothering about breakfast."

"Then let's us go downstairs to the dining room. We'll have ourselves some breakfast and then I want to go have a talk with your father. I want to find out exactly where he spotted Wildfire."

"My parents are staying here in the hotel," Violet informed Sutton. "Suppose we go up to their room. Perhaps they will join us for breakfast."

"Good idea. That way we can kill two birds with one stone."

They took the elevator to the floor on which the Wilsons had their room. Violet knocked on their door which was opened by a collarless Ronald Wilson who was in the midst of a yawn. The yawn dissipated when he saw that one of his early morning visitors was Sutton.

"Violet," he said. "I bid you good day. To what do I owe this early morning call, may I ask?"

"Mr. Wilson," Sutton began, "you have yourself a very persuasive daughter."

"Persuasive?"

Violet could not contain herself. "Father, I just called on Luke and I've managed to convince him to change his mind and try to capture Wildfire for you."

"Is that true, Mr. Sutton?" Wilson asked, his eyes widening.

"It is," Sutton answered.

"Upon my word!" Wilson exclaimed and then hurriedly ushered Sutton and Violet into the room where a fully dressed Mrs. Wilson sat in an overstuffed chair.

Sutton paid her his compliments and then, responding to Wilson's many questions, which tumbled excitedly from the man's lips, he said, "Violet and I were just about to have ourselves some breakfast. We thought maybe you two would want to join us."

"Breakfast?" Wilson spluttered. "Who has time for breakfast?"

"We do, my dear," Mrs. Wilson said calmly as she rose, picked up a paper collar from the dresser, and proceeded to fasten it to her husband's shirt. "Now where did you put your cravat, Ronald?"

Ten minutes later the foursome was seated at a choice table in the hotel's dining room. Five minutes after taking their places, they were served grape juice, scrambled eggs, thick slices of ham, coffee, and buttered white bread warm from the oven.

Wilson made an effort to eat but finally gave it up. He put down his fork and exclaimed, "By Jove, Mr. Sutton, I am a happy man this morning, thanks to you."

"Whatever did you do, darling, to make Mr. Sutton change his mind?" Mrs. Wilson asked her daughter.

Violet explained what had happened during her earlier meeting with Sutton.

"Outrageous!" Wilson roared when she had finished her account. "Why, to think that anyone would be so foolhardy as to want to destroy that marvelous stallion! I *can't* think it. It's *un*thinkable!"

"Mr. Wilson," Sutton said, "where exactly was it that you spotted the stallion? Do you know?"

"Well, I am not familiar with Nevada, as you might suppose," Wilson replied. "But after I saw the horse I made inquiries of the stage driver while we were stopped at the stage station, which was, incidentally, called Brewster's Rest. He told me about the range he was wont to roam with his mares and foals.

"The sighting took place in the eastern part of the state—Eureka County, to be specific about it. The stage driver told me that we were then on the west side of Pine Valley and that the horse herd roamed the north-south-running mountain range in that area. Do you happen to be familiar with that part of the state, Mr. Sutton?"

"I traveled through there once but I can't claim it as a stamping ground of mine. I stayed for a short spell out there in a little mountain town name of Palisade. That mountain range you mentioned, it's one big happy hunting ground for men with mustang fever."

"And it will soon be the same for the army and stud killers out to collect bounties," Wilson added dolefully. Then, brightening, "I am glad to hear though that the area is not unknown to you. That should help to make your job a bit easier."

"Being familiar with the lay of the land might help me," Sutton agreed. "But those mountains are chockfull of canyons and hidden valleys that make choice places where a horse herd can hide from mustangers.

Eureka County's not much settled, which is another thing that makes it ideal ground for a horse herd. As a rule, the herds stay up in the high country at elevations anywhere from six to nine thousand feet. Summertimes, like now, they forage on bunch grass, but after the first killing frost comes they make do with white sage."

"Listen to him, my dear!" Wilson cried happily, addressing his wife, who had finished her breakfast and was delicately patting her lips with a linen napkin. "He sounds like he was born and raised in those mountains, doesn't he? And as far as knowing horses and their habits—I am more than ever convinced I have picked the right man for the job. Which reminds me."

Wilson took a purse from his pocket, opened it, counted out some folding money, and offered it to Sutton. "There is one thousand dollars here," he said. "Half the agreed-upon fee. I will pay you the balance upon the successful completion of your mission, Mr. Sutton, if that is acceptable to you."

Sutton shook his head.

"You want all the money now?" Wilson inquired, frowning.

Sutton shook his head again. "It's been my policy, Mr. Wilson, to collect my fee when—and only if—I succeed in what I set out to do."

"When do you plan to leave, Luke?" Violet asked.

"Today," he answered to Wilson's obvious delight. "There's an eastbound stage set to leave town at noon."

"I must say, Mr. Sutton," Mrs. Wilson remarked with something like awe in her voice, "you don't let any grass grow under your feet."

"I told you, Mother," Violet said brightly. "Once Luke makes up his mind to do something there is simply no stopping him. He'll brook neither delays nor interference."

"When will you return?" her father asked Sutton.

"Can't answer that one for you," Sutton replied. "It could take me days, once I get to where I'm going, or it could take me weeks to catch Wildfire. Why'd you ask? Does that pose a problem for you?"

Wilson hesitated a moment before answering. "Well, I don't like being away from my business for too long a time except under unusual circumstances. But this is certainly not only an unusual but a quite exceptional circumstance, isn't it? I'll wire my men that my return will be indefinitely delayed. I'm sure they can manage things in my absence. I'll tell them to contact me here at the hotel if necessary. You take what time you need. Time is not the critical element in this venture. Its success is. I'll await your return here at the hotel."

"Well, if you'll excuse me," Sutton said. He drank the last of his coffee and then rose, picking up the check. "Good day to you, ladies." He shook hands with Wilson, who wished him the best of luck, and then, after paying the check, he returned to his room where he proceeded to get ready for the journey that lay ahead.

When Sutton appeared at the stage station at eleven forty-five that morning, he was wearing a brown bib shirt beneath a leather vest, faded jeans tucked into his black army boots, a tan bandanna around his neck, and, on his head, a flat-topped black Stetson.

Around his hips was strapped a leather cartridge belt which had a shell in each of its loops. In the oiled holster that hung from the belt was a six-shot Remington Army Revolver, Model 1875, caliber .45.

He carried a bedroll, canteen, lariat, his saddle and

bridle, and a Winchester '73 in a saddle boot. After paying his fare to Brewster's Rest, the stage station that Wilson had mentioned to him, he placed his gear in the boot beneath the stage driver's seat.

Fifteen minutes later, the driver of the stage announced to his six assembled passengers that he was ready to leave. There was a flurry of skirts as two women boarded the stage, followed by four men who were also making the journey, Sutton among the latter.

As a result of a judicious push here and shove there, Sutton succeeded in seating himself on the benchlike seat at the rear of the coach, which had been his goal; there he wouldn't have to face those passengers ensconced on the middle seat and sitting practically nose to nose with the passengers on the third seat, who had their backs to the front of the coach.

With a loud yell and a crack of his whip, the driver set the six horses moving and soon they were trotting at a steady pace. The coach swayed and at times threatened to overturn. But just before that disaster could occur, the driver would yell at the top of his lungs, *"Right!"* or *"Left!"* and the passengers would all lean either to the right or to the left as directed, in order to counterbalance the dangerously leaning coach and thus prevent it from winding up on its side.

They made their first stop a little more than an hour after their journey had begun, and their second stop an hour and a half after that.

Sutton endured the discomfort that he knew was an inevitable part of a journey by stagecoach—the lurching, bouncing, and tilting first to one side, then to the other, then forward, then backward, as the coach hit a rut or a stone in the road or traveled over a stretch of ground that was less a road than a deer path ambling through the woods. His body was soon aching, its lower half mercifully numb. But his head, despite his persistent attempts to shield it, suffered most. When the coach bounced, his head, like those of the other passengers, sometimes struck the roof of the coach, flattening his hat but not quite cracking his skull.

One of the men on the front seat leaned to one side so he could see to the rear past the two women perched on the middle seat, and asked Sutton where he was headed.

"East," Sutton answered noncommittally.

"Well, that's plain as day, mister," responded the questioner. "We're all of us heading east to one place or another. Me and Billy here, we're heading for White Pine County. We mean to make us some money once we get there. Ain't that a fact, Billy?"

Billy grinned and nodded enthusiastically. "We plan on shooting us some horses once we get to where it is we're going. They're paying ten dollars a horse hide, I hear."

"I do declare!" cried one of the women. "Whoever heard of such a thing as shooting horses? Horses shouldn't be shot. They're valuable property. Why, you could get yourselves arrested!" she admonished Billy and his companion.

"Oh, we're not going to shoot any horse what belongs to somebody," Billy quickly assured her. "Ain't you heard about how some cattle ranchers have been offering a bounty for every unbranded wild horse a man can kill?"

Billy's companion, after drawing aside the leather window shade he had earlier lowered to stop most of the trail dust stirred up by the coach from blowing into it, spat and added, "I just hope we get there in time and we ain't too late. I hear men—not to mention boys not yet old enough to go courting—are flocking to the mountains east of here to earn bounty money by shooting down as many wild horses as they can find."

Sutton pulled his Stetson down over his eyes, folded his arms across his chest, and tried to sleep. He couldn't. Just about the time he would begin to doze, the coach would hit something in the road and he would be jostled awake. He nevertheless maintained his position in order to discourage Billy and his colleague from continuing their conversation about killing wild horses. Their words had brought to his mind a vivid and unsettling image of the golden hide of Wildfire lying limp in a heap on the ground while the stud's bloody carcass lay steaming beside it in the cool mountain air.

The remainder of the journey was punctuated by stops made every twelve to twenty miles at stage stations, most of which were primitive establishments like the one where the passengers and driver made their nooning. Sutton ate with the driver at a table next to and touching at one end a thin partition. Behind it, he could hear the snorting of horses. When one of the animals kicked the partition, the dishes on the table rattled.

"How you bearing up under the strain?" the driver asked Sutton once he had finished eating every scrap of food on his plate.

"About as well as can be expected."

"I know coach travel is a far piece from comfortable," the driver offered, and belched contentedly. Placing both hands, fingers interlocked, on his bulging belly, he added, "But it gets you where you want to go —and usually in one piece too." He gave a shrill giggle, obviously amused by his crude attempt at humor.

"The days aren't so bad," Sutton said. "But the

nights—as I recall from other times I've taken long rides like this one on a stagecoach—the nights are hell with the lights out."

"You said a mouthful, mister! And you're right. Trying to get some sleep on a stage is a forlorn hope—a little like trying to catch yourself some Saint Anthony's fire."

When Sutton had finished his meal, he went outside where the two ladies were attempting to freshen up at the half-filled wash basin that sat on a bench just outside the door. When they had used their handkerchief to try to clean their faces and hands, they surveyed the unsatisfactory results in a cracked mirror that hung above the basin on the wall of the building. Then one of them, with a resigned sigh and a shrug, used the comb that hung on a cord from a nail next to the mirror and which was full of accumulated hair of many lengths and colors.

The journey resumed.

It ended for Sutton late the following afternoon when the coach pulled up at Brewster's Rest. He got out and retrieved his gear from the boot. Inside the log building, he spoke to the proprietor of the station who identified himself as Jim Brewster.

"I'm looking to buy me a horse," he told Brewster. "A good strong horse. You happen to have one for sale?"

"I have more than one," Brewster replied. "A stage station like this has to have more horses than a cow flop has flies, considering the business we're in. We buy them off mustangers who work this part of the country."

"I'd like to take a look at your stock if I might."

"They're out back in the corral. Don't waste your time with the ones in the barn. They're stage stock and not for sale. I'll be back to join you once I finish switching the horses on the coach."

Sutton went around the side of the building to the corral, in which close to a dozen mustangs were penned. He hooked a boot on the lowest pole of the corral, spread his forearms on another pole, and studied the stock. He immediately dismissed a roan with a lame leg and a pinto with a narrow brisket. The horses, he noted, were an odd assortment. He spotted an Appaloosa with its leopard-spotted hide, an animal that probably had an ancestry reaching back to Turkey or Spain. There was a palomino of a paler gold than Wildfire was supposed to be, and a gaudily spotted thirteen-hands-high horse, brown on white. Both of the latter had badly tangled manes reaching almost to their hocks, a sure sign of their formerly wild lives. One of them was bizarrely humpbacked; it reminded Sutton of the tales he had heard told of the time when camels ran wild on Nevada's ranges and, legend had it, interbred with the wild mustangs.

By the time Brewster had rejoined him following the departure of the stage, Sutton had more or less settled on a black with a blaze and four white feet.

"Seen anything that suits you?" Brewster asked him.

Sutton pointed to the black. "Is he green broke?"

"More or less."

Sutton, not liking the sound of the response, glanced at Brewster who shrugged and said, "Just about each and every one of those fuzztails you see there are broke to one degree or another. But it's also true that just about each and every one of them has some wildness left in them."

"I notice the black's wearing only three shoes. How come?"

"Been meaning to get around to replacing the shoe

he threw," Brewster droned. "Just haven't found the time."

"I'll be wanting him to have all of his shoes—if we can agree on a price after I've taken a closer look at him."

"You're welcome to do the job yourself, mister. There's a forge in that tack shed yonder."

Sutton gave Brewster an appraising look. "The fact is you've not been able to handle him, isn't it? That's why he's only got three shoes on him. He didn't throw one. Am I right?"

"I'm not aiming to cheat you, mister. Yes, that's the truth. So maybe you'd best settle on some other horse. That there black, he's a demon. A biter and a kicker."

"He has spirit, does he?"

"Oh, he has spirit in spades, yes sirree. Enough to eat a man like you for breakfast and spit out all his bones."

Sutton picked up a halter that was draped over one of the corral's poles and went inside the enclosure. He made his way over to where the black was standing his ground, while the other horses wheeled warily out of his path. When he reached the black, he quickly put on the halter. Then, as he started to lead the horse over to where Brewster was standing, the black snapped at him. Because he had been warned that the horse was a biter, Sutton was prepared for the ploy. Swiftly, he punched the black between the eyes with his right fist before its teeth could make contact with him.

Undeterred by the blow, the black tried a second time to bite and for his trouble received another swift blow from Sutton's clenched fist, also between the eyes. When the horse tried for a third time, the mere sight of Sutton's fist flashing upward and prepared to strike caused the black to swing his head to one side and make no further attacks.

When he had rejoined Brewster outside the corral, Sutton carefully examined the horse he had chosen. He checked its teeth, which told him the animal was two to three years old. His legs were sound, and his brisket was broad, suggesting that the horse had good wind.

"How much?" he asked Brewster.

"Fifteen dollars."

"For fifteen dollars I'd not expect to have to be my own blacksmith and put a shoe on him."

"You finish shoeing him and I'll knock another dollar off the price. I bet he won't try biting you again. Not after the way you almost stopped his clock with that fist of yours."

"I'll give you eleven for him."

Five minutes later they agreed on a price of twelve-fifty, which Sutton paid. Then he took the black to the tack shed where he tied it to an upright and proceeded to heat the forge. When the forge was glowing a bright cherry red, he began to shape the piece of iron he had gripped in the tongs with a hammer. When it was ready, he plunged it into a barrel of water and watched as steam hissed up from the hot metal.

He tried lifting the horse's hind leg to scrape its hoof into a shape to receive the shoe, but as he did so the black jerked backward, almost pulling the upright loose and bringing the roof down upon himself and Sutton.

Letting go of the horse's leg, Sutton decided to construct a twitch to help him control the black. He reached for a broom that was leaning against the wall. He broke its handle in half and then, taking the upper half of the handle, he pounded a nail through its rounded end. After withdrawing the nail, he threaded a stout cord through the hole he had made, to create a loop about six inches in diameter. He put his hand through the loop, pulled out the horse's upper lip, and with his free hand slid the twitch he had made on the lip; then, taking a horseshoe down from the wall, he used one of its branches to twist the cord tight.

When he was satisfied that it was tight enough, he slipped one branch of the shoe through the side ring in the halter to hold the cord in place, and then proceeded to apply the shoe he had made. He had no further trouble from the black, who stood stiff-legged in reaction to the twitch binding its upper lip.

Fifteen minutes later he had his gear on the black; then, after a meal of fried potatoes and roasted venison served to him by Brewster, he bid the proprietor of the stage station good-bye.

As he climbed into the saddle and put heels to the black, the horse suddenly pitched, nearly throwing him to the ground. When the horse prepared to repeat his performance, Sutton slammed his fist down on top of the animal's head.

The black quickly gentled.

Sutton moved him out, heading north.

THREE

SUTTON RODE SLOWLY NORTH, his eyes roving across the mountainous land he was moving through. The area was full of wildlife—he spotted deer, grouse, wild turkeys, rabbits. Crows cawed their way across the sky they briefly shared with a gliding golden eagle. A snarl that became a short-lived scream told Sutton that there was a cougar in the vicinity, although he could not see it.

His black pranced nervously in response to the shrill sound. It tossed its head, apparently catching the cougar's scent on the breeze that was causing the tree branches to sway and Sutton's hair to lift off his collar.

He crested a ridge, both slopes of which were covered with blue spruce trees, and started down the other side, moving among the trees on a necessarily irregular course, ducking now and then as sudden strong gusts of wind sent low-hanging branches sweeping toward him. When he came to a stream, he drew rein, dismounted, and filled his canteen with cold water.

An hour later he was fording a deeper stream, in a shallow valley with mountain peaks all around, when he heard what sounded like still-distant thunder but was not thunder, he knew, not on such a sunny day with few clouds in the sky.

He listened for a moment until he had identified the direction from which the sound was coming, the sound he was sure was being made by the hooves of horses—an entire herd of them. He drew rein and sat his saddle as the sound gradually grew louder. Then he moved into the shadows beneath some leafy white birch trees.

The black beneath him moved restlessly. He patted its neck and whispered to it but the horse still fidgeted. It nickered when a horse herd topped the ridge on Sutton's right and came pounding down its slope into the valley below. Through the dust that was being raised by the herd, Sutton strained his eyes to see whether Wildfire was among the mustangs that had begun to wheel around the valley in a great circle, as if they were reconnoitering it. He saw no animal that matched the stallion's description. He nevertheless continued examining the individual animals in the herd in case he just might have missed seeing the legendary stud. Wildfire, he was soon sure, was not one of the herd, which was composed, according to his quick count, of about twenty mares, seven foals, and a single stallion.

The herd gradually slowed and then stopped their circling. They milled for several minutes, the dappled stallion circling them and occasionally nipping the necks or flanks of mares who strayed too far from the main body of the herd. Then, apparently satisfied with the valley, the herd began to graze on the grass that grew so abundantly on its flat floor.

Sutton was about to leave his refuge among the birches when he heard a scream that he knew had not been made by the cougar he had heard earlier. This scream, he knew, had been made by a horse. But not, he was also sure, by any of the herd newly gathered in the valley.

He looked up and saw a huge stallion skylined on a

ridge. He was transfixed by the sight of the huge animal standing so regally, like an apparition that was above and not of the mundane world spread out far below it. Its hide gleamed golden in the sun. Even when, for a brief moment, the sun vanished behind a cloud, the stallion Sutton was convinced was Wildfire seemed to glow in the diffused light. The horse's mane was long and also golden. Its body was perfectly proportioned, and Sutton estimated the horse stood at least fifteen, perhaps sixteen, hands high.

The stallion pawed the ground with its right front hoof. It screamed again and then went racing down from the ridge, heading for the valley below.

Sutton lost sight of the mustang as it galloped into a stand of timber but he could hear it, hear the whistle it was emitting, a rarely heard sound, one that he had heard only twice before in his life. It was made when a horse blew sharply and loudly through its nostrils, and it carried a considerable distance.

Suppressing the urge to set out after the golden stallion, Sutton forced himself instead to sit his saddle and wait. He did not want to find himself in the midst of the fight that he was sure was coming. To be caught between two battling studs, each of them weighing a thousand pounds or more, could, he knew, turn him into mincemeat. He bided his time.

The challenging stallion emerged from the trees and raced down onto the floor of the valley, where he halted not far from the herd's stallion. He began then what was to Sutton a familiar ritual, one he had witnessed several times before in his earlier days as a mustanger.

The lone stallion began to strut belligerently, feinting at his rival, the herd-master. He tossed his head. He pawed the ground. He feinted again, moving in on the herd's stallion and then stepping adroitly to one side as the horse he was challenging gave a scream of rage and bared its teeth, which glistened wetly in the bright sunlight.

The golden stallion reared up on his hind legs and came down hard, his left front hoof striking the other stallion a solid blow on the shoulder that sent him to his knees. Seizing his advantage, the attacker also dropped to his knees and dug his teeth into the other horse's right hock.

As the attacked stud tried to rise, his opponent vigorously shook his head, still biting down hard on the stud's hock, trying, Sutton was certain, to tear a tendon in order to hamstring his adversary.

The downed stallion screamed, and in the sound was naked rage and pain. Then it bit its attacker's neck, bloodying the animal's mane, jerked free, and leaped to its feet. It moved warily to one side, still facing its opponent who had also risen, searching for an opening.

The herd-master moved to the other side, a surprisingly graceful ballet that embodied a clear threat. Suddenly it lowered its head and charged the challenger, who met the onslaught by again dropping to its knees, lowering its head, and baring its teeth. The maneuver tumbled the herd-master to the ground, all four legs waving helplessly for a moment. But it quickly recovered and once again both horses resumed the battle, their teeth bared and their eyes blazing as they feinted, snapped, screamed, and strutted arrogantly to display their courage.

As the struggle continued and each combatant succeeded in both biting and kicking its opponent, the mares, as if sensing that they were the prize the two studs were fighting over, stood docilely in a group as they awaited the outcome of the battle.

Sutton began to wonder whether he had made a wise decision in staying clear of the encounter. That herd stud's liable to kill my quarry—if that golden stud really is Wildfire, he thought. Blood now matted the golden stallion's mane, and he was limping slightly because he had been bitten twice on the leg. He's no good to Wilson dead, Sutton thought, tightening his grip on his reins. On the other hand, he reminded himself, studs like those two big fellows don't generally fight to the death. That's just not nature's way. What's happening here, he thought, is a fight over territory, or I miss my guess. Sooner or later, one of those two horses is going to give up and wander off. But which one? And when?

He was so engrossed in watching the raging battle between the two titans that he didn't hear the rider come up behind him. Only when she spoke did he realize he was no longer alone.

"Which one do you think will win?"

Sutton turned to find a young woman sitting her saddle just behind him.

Before he could answer the question she had asked him, she said, "It's really no contest. Wildfire will win."

"How do, miss," he said, touching the brim of his hat as she moved up beside him. "I kind of figured that stud was Wildfire, though I couldn't be positive about it."

"Oh yes, that's him. This is part of his home range— this valley, these mountains." She pointed to the east. "He is very territorial. He won't let any other stallion try to take what belongs to him."

Sutton, studying the woman beside him, decided

that she was about twenty years old. Her hair was a glossy auburn which reflected the sunlight. Her blue eyes were serious as they watched the continuing struggle between the two horses. She's more than just good-looking, he decided. She's only a step or two away from being beautiful.

"Look," she said, "it's over."

Sutton turned his attention back to the two horses and found that the woman was right. The fight was over. Wildfire followed the stallion he had vanquished for a short distance, his head down as he nipped at the departing loser's hocks. The beaten stud leaned to one side, making Sutton believe that the animal had suffered a dislocated shoulder. He's done for, he thought. He won't have a chance to get his mares back now, not with the shape Wildfire's left him in.

"Well," he said aloud, as Wildfire turned and headed back to the mares, bunching and biting them and beginning to drive them toward the slope that led to the ridge he had come down from earlier, "it's clear who the winner of that go-round is."

The woman nodded.

"It was nice talking to you, miss," Sutton said, "but if you'll excuse me now, I've got to be on my way." Without waiting for a response, he moved his black out and into a fast gallop. He set off in pursuit of Wildfire, who was squealing and ramming his captured mares and their foals as he drove them up the slope.

He used his reins as a whip to urge his black into greater and then still greater speed. Gradually, he closed the distance between himself and the herd Wildfire had appropriated. He rode directly behind the stallion, hoping to get as close to him as possible before the animal realized he was being pursued. He believed he had a good chance of coming abreast of

Wildfire before the horse knew he was being hunted, because the animal was totally involved with the herding of his captured mares.

The plan might have worked but for the fact that, when Sutton was still some distance away from his target, a mare suddenly made a break for freedom. An instant after she had veered to the right and gone racing away from the herd, Wildfire turned and went after her. He had not gone more than a few yards when he spotted Sutton, who had swerved in his direction.

Wildfire whistled angrily and abandoned his pursuit of the renegade mare. He wheeled and, tossing his great head, galloped back to where the mares he had captured were slowing down, a few of them already stopped and beginning to bunch.

That's it, Sutton thought with glee. You keep your mind on your ladies and I'll have me a whole lot better chance of catching you. Chuckling, he turned and rode back the way he had come. You'll not be the first stud, animal or human, to be undone by the ladies, he silently told his quarry.

Wildfire screamed when he reached the mares. He butted one of them with his head, sending her flying up the slope, the others nearby pacing her in their renewed alarm. Then the stallion raced to the rear of the herd where he again rammed the laggards with the full brute force of his huge body. They responded by defensively leaping and rearing and then racing up the slope. Wildfire's head turned sharply in Sutton's direction. Then, capering as if to taunt his pursuer, he rounded the rear of the herd and disappeared on its opposite side.

"Damnation!" Sutton muttered. By standing up in his stirrups, he was able to catch a glimpse of the golden mustang on the far side of the herd. One thing's for sure, he thought. That horse is no dummy. He's put the mares between him and me and I swear he did it on purpose. But I'm not whipped yet.

He slowed his black. Then he tightened his grip on the reins and his mount slowed even more. When the last of the mares had bisected his trail, he put heels to his horse and again went galloping after his prey. As he came parallel to the rear end of the herd, he turned his black and resumed his pursuit of Wildfire, who was directly ahead of him now and separated from him by no more than twenty yards.

He reached for his rope as he rode. Minutes later, he was beside Wildfire. The horse turned its head, bared its teeth, and snorted several times. Sutton fashioned a loop and whirled it above his head. Then, carefully judging the distance and speed of the stallion, he let the lariat fly.

Wildfire, with another snort that Sutton was ready to swear sounded contemptuous, slammed into the mare running on his right, toppling her to the ground. The barrier her fallen body formed caused a pileup of several mares and a foal which had been running directly behind her.

Sutton drew in his lariat, which had failed to snare the prize he had been aiming for because of the way Wildfire had evaded the rope: moving in among the mares and thereby making himself a more difficult target.

Sutton moved his black in among the herd, one hand stiffly gripping his saddle horn to help him stay in the saddle amidst the jostling and pounding of tons of horseflesh all around him. He managed to make his way up alongside Wildfire once more. This time he had the horse on his left as they crested the ridge and started down it toward another herd of mares, bunched in the mouth of a canyon below.

If he gets into the middle of those two bunches, Sutton thought grimly, I'll never again get near enough to him to rope him. He transferred his coiled lariat from his right to his left hand and then struck Wildfire across the nose with it. The stallion seemed not to feel the blow, or at least he was undeterred from his course, which had been Sutton's reason for striking him—to turn him out of the herd and make him an easier target for the lariat.

Sutton struck again. But it wasn't until the fourth such strike that Wildfire succumbed to the punishment and lurched to the side. Sutton intensified his strikes, careful to avoid the horse's eyes but determined to press the advantage he had gained. Moments later he had succeeded in driving Wildfire from the herd of mares, which continued on their downward course. They headed toward the other mares, who seemed to be waiting for them at the mouth of the canyon below.

Whirling his lariat above his head, he swung a wide loop. When he was close enough, almost parallel to Wildfire, he let the loop go. He swore when the mustang suddenly slackened his pace just enough to dodge behind Sutton's black. Sutton's lariat fell empty to the ground. Wildfire, behind Sutton, whistled as he fled back the way he had come, to rejoin the mares.

Sutton wheeled his mount and, swearing, set out after the stallion again, determined this time not to be outfoxed by the wily horse which, he had to admit, he had begun to admire for the clever and intelligent tactics it had employed to avoid being captured.

This time he was not outfoxed by the horse but by the woman he had briefly met earlier.

He shouted a warning to her when he spotted her angling across the slope toward him, riding, as he phrased it to himself, hell-bent for election. If she held to her course and to her pace, and if he did also, they were sure to collide.

"Get out of the way!" he yelled at the top of his voice, waving his lariat as if he could drive her from his path by the gesture.

She did not turn but kept coming relentlessly toward him. He forced his black to give him more speed. But the additional speed the horse delivered on command did not help. He was not able to outdistance the woman who was coming at him from a right angle as if she were determined to run him down. He realized that there was only one thing he could do to save himself from the inevitable consequences of the foolhardy course the woman was following, for reasons he could not even begin to understand.

Giving up the chase, he turned his black, of necessity, so sharply that the iron bit in the horse's mouth almost ripped the animal's lips. For a moment he was riding away from the oncoming woman, and then he wheeled in a tight circle and rode up behind her. When he had caught up with her, he reached out, seized her horse's bridle, and brought her mount to a sudden and stiff-legged halt.

"What the Sam Hill were you trying to do?" he bellowed at her.

She sat her saddle, sweat adding a sheen to her face, and stared at him without answering.

"You could have killed me the way you were riding, don't you know that? You could have killed yourself along with me. What in the world possessed you?"

"Love," she answered calmly, despite her breathlessness.

Sutton let go of the bridle. It was his turn to stare at her, and stare he did in utter and complete bewilderment. "Love," he repeated. He reached up, pushed his hat back on his head, and grunted. "Are you loco, lady?"

"Not in the least. As a matter of fact, I consider myself not only sane but a good deal more sensible than most men of your ilk."

"My ilk? What do you mean by 'my ilk'?"

"Stud killers. That's what I mean."

"I'm no stud killer. Whatever gave you the idea I was a stud killer?"

Her eyes widened in surprise and then narrowed in apparent disbelief. "You're armed." She pointed to his side arm and then to the Winchester in its saddle boot. "You were hunting Wildfire."

"I wasn't hunting him if you mean trying to kill him. I was chasing him, yes, but not hunting him. The fact that I wear a gun and carry a rifle don't make me a stud killer."

"You're not one of those terrible men then?"

"I already told you I'm not."

"I still don't believe you."

"I don't give a hoot whether you believe me or not. I told you the truth and you can take it or you can leave it, it makes not one damn bit of difference to me which you decide to do."

"I saw you strike Wildfire with your rope. I saw you trying to blind him with it. You can't deny that."

"I don't deny it! I was trying to turn him. It's a way mustangers have of turning a horse. You use a rope or a quirt if you've got one. But I wasn't trying to blind him; I just wanted to turn him out of the herd."

"Why?"

"I wanted to get my rope on him."

"That's almost as bad. In fact, it is as bad."

"Now what are you talking about?"

"Simply this. To catch and corral a horse like Wildfire is tantamount to imposing a death sentence on him. He couldn't live penned up, not him. He'd die of a broken heart. So to catch him would be the same, although admittedly not nearly as dramatic, as to shoot and kill him."

Sutton wearily took off his hat and wiped his sweaty forehead with the back of his hand. Shaking his head, he said, "What did you mean before when I asked you what possessed you and you said 'love'?"

"I meant that I acted to prevent you from killing— or, as you claim, catching—Wildfire out of love for the horse and all others like him. I don't want to see him caught. When I realized what you were going to do— alright, maybe I was wrong about your being a stud killer. But I *believed* you were at the time and so I made up my mind to save Wildfire in the only way I could. By riding down on you and forcing you to let him alone."

Sutton gazed off into the distance. "Well, I'll say this for you. You got done just exactly what you set out to do."

A look of triumph spread across the woman's face. "Yes, it does seem so, doesn't it?"

Sutton glared at her. He shook a finger in her face. "But I'll get him, you can count on that. And not even a half-dozen bleeding-heart ladies such as yourself will stop me from getting him neither."

Tears suddenly appeared in the woman's eyes. She bit her lower lip.

Sutton, no longer glaring at her, asked, "What's wrong?"

She looked away from him, brushing furiously at a tear that slid down her cheek.

"What's wrong?" he repeated.

"The fact that you're probably right in what you say, that's what's wrong. I just happened to be here today and saw what you were trying to do. Fortunately, I was able to stop you. But I won't always be here to stop you. So it's probably true that you will be able to catch Wildfire someday and there will not be a thing I can do to stop you."

As the woman started to ride away, Sutton went after her. Once again, he seized her horse's bridle, halting her.

"Let me go!" she demanded. "Don't you have better things to do than to carry on a conversation with a lady who might be loco? Things such as breaking the heart of a horse like Wildfire by catching and confining him?"

Sutton kept his grip on the bridle as he answered, "I'm here to do that horse a favor."

The woman turned angry eyes on him.

"You're way too quick to jump to judgement, lady. And you're not very logical into the bargain."

"I don't know what you mean nor do I care to."

"What I mean, it's this. You yourself said there are stud killers out after mustangs like Wildfire and his herd. Well, I'm out to catch that horse like I already told you. If you look at it one way, by catching him I'll be keeping him alive and safe from all the stud killers and the ranchers who want to rid the world of every last wild horse God gave life to. Think about that for a minute or two, lady."

She was silent for a long moment. Then, "You intend to break him—turn him into a saddle horse?"

"I intend to break him, yes. I don't intend to turn

him into what I reckon is your notion of a saddle horse."

"Please explain yourself."

Sutton proceeded to tell the woman about having been commissioned by Ronald Wilson to find, catch, and break Wildfire for him so that he could use the stallion in his breeding and racing programs.

When he had finished, the woman said, "I still think Wildfire should be let live a life of freedom."

"He hasn't got such a good chance of doing that," Sutton countered, "if some stud killer puts a bullet in his brain, now has he?"

With evident reluctance, the woman shook her head.

"He'll have a good life with Mr. Wilson, Wildfire will," Sutton continued. "Mr. Wilson will take good care of him. Wildfire'll do just fine back East. What's more important is he'll be alive."

A dreamy expression drifted across the woman's face as she gazed in the direction the vanished horse herd had taken. "I sometimes think I would like to catch Wildfire myself. Take him away from here to someplace where no one would want to hurt him—not for money, not for any reason.

"But what can I, a woman, do? Oh, I'm a good horse-woman. But I could never catch an animal like Wildfire. Even if I could, I couldn't control him. So my dream has always been just that—a dream."

"Maybe I can make it come true for you."

The woman turned expectantly to Sutton.

He said, "I'm going to do—if I can without nobody interfering with me—what you dream of doing. I'm going to rope Wildfire and take him to a place where he'll be safe."

"I still wish he could remain wild and not be caught and broken."

"To tell you the truth, I feel pretty much the same way. It took some fancy talking to get me to agree to come out here after Wildfire. I felt at first like you do —that Wildfire ought to be let free to roam like the wind. But Mr. Wilson—or rather his daughter, Violet —used the same argument on me that I just used on you. Violet pointed out to me that Wildfire stood himself a good chance of getting killed if I didn't catch him first and get him out of harm's way."

"I'm surprised, quite frankly, to hear you say you would prefer to let the wild horses remain wild. All the men I know either want to kill them or break and sell them."

"I was a mustanger myself once down in Texas," Sutton said. "But after I'd spent some time in jail I learned to value my freedom. Maybe that's why I wasn't exactly ready to jump when Mr. Wilson first made me his proposition."

The woman was looking at Sutton with interest. "May I know your name?"

"It's Sutton. Lucas Sutton. Folks call me Luke unless they're riled at me, and I won't tell you what they call me then."

The woman smiled. "My name is Judith Fletcher. I suppose I don't have to say it but I will anyway. Even without me to interfere in your efforts to capture Wildfire, you are facing a very difficult task. That stallion is as clever as he is intelligent. He'll give you a good run for your money. Good day to you, Mr. Sutton."

Sutton touched the brim of his hat to Judith and watched her ride off. Then he turned his horse and rode up to the ridge. Looking down from his vantage point, he saw no sign of Wildfire or his mares and foals.

He rode down from the ridge to the mouth of the canyon where the mares he had seen earlier had been bunched. On the way, he picked up the trail of the mares Wildfire had captured from the other herd-master. When he reached level ground, he began to follow their trail, hoping to come upon them—and Wildfire—again.

He had not been riding long when he heard the un-mistakable sound of hoofbeats in the distance ahead of him. Moments later he saw the first of what turned out to be between ten and twenty mares round a bend and come thundering into view.

He moved out of their path and as he did so he spotted the rider behind the horses, half hidden by the dust the small herd was raising. The man was flogging his mount with a quirt as he galloped after the horses.

Sutton felt a pang of regret as he watched the man. When he had first heard the sound of hoofbeats, he had hoped that what he was hearing was the sound of Wildfire and his herd returning. But Wildfire was not among the mares fleeing the pursuing rider.

When the mares, as if in response to some unseen signal, suddenly parted into two smaller herds, one going to the left, the other to the right, Sutton moved swiftly out, intending to help the man, who was obviously a mustanger, round up the scattering horses.

But, as he closed in on half of the herd and was about to try to turn them, the mustanger let out an indignant roar and then shouted, "Them's my mares, mister! You leave 'em be!"

FOUR

"I'M NOT AFTER YOUR HORSES," Sutton yelled, but his words were lost in the pounding sound made by the scores of hooves hitting the ground.

He rode on beside the mustanger in pursuit of one part of the split-up herd. As he did so, the mustanger began to move in on him from the left. His horse first crowded and then bumped Sutton's mount.

Sutton moved his horse away to avoid the other horse. "I take it," he yelled at the top of his voice, "you don't want me to lend you a hand."

The other man didn't answer—not in words. He raised the quirt he had in his right hand and brought it sharply down on Sutton's shoulders.

Pain streaked through Sutton's flesh at the harsh touch of the braided leather. He swore aloud and, when the man next to him once again raised the quirt to strike another blow, he reached out, wrested the weapon from the man's raised hand, and threw it to the ground, still swearing.

At the same time, he drew rein and brought his black to a sudden halt. The horse circled, causing him to lose sight momentarily of the mustanger. When he had managed to steady his mount, he still could not see the other man, who was lost in the billowing dust that had been raised by the fleeing horses. The sound of the animals was fading fast as Sutton swore again, damning himself for having tried to be a good Samaritan.

What the hell did it get me, he asked himself. Nothing but a mouthful of dust and about as much fun as a baby with a bellyache can have. Let him have his herd and may it make him as happy as a pig in a peach orchard.

He was just about to turn his horse and continue his hunt for Wildfire when he caught a glimpse of the mustanger in the distance. The man was still riding hard directly behind the part of the herd he had been chasing. He began moving into it, neatly splitting it as if he and his horse were a cleaver. But the maneuver, whatever its intent had been, did not work. The horses on either side of the mustanger swung their heads and snapped viciously at his mount, as if the horse and not its rider was their enemy. The attacked horse screamed as it was bitten repeatedly. Its gait changed. Then, balking, it tried to get out from between the two wild horses flanking it. As it did so, it reared and its rider lost his balance. His feet flew out of the stirrups and, as his horse's hooves hit the ground, he lost his grip on the reins and was thrown backward out of the saddle.

He had barely hit the ground when one of the horses that had attacked his mount turned and began racing back the way it had come, toward where the mustanger lay motionless on the ground.

Sutton swiftly moved his horse out and into a ground-pounding gallop. He went racing toward the fallen man. As he came closer to him, he stood up in his stirrups and began yelling at the top of his voice in an effort to first attract the wild horse's attention, and then to turn the animal and send it back to the herd before it could do any damage to the man on the ground.

But, when his shouting did nothing to deter the

horse, he began to fear that he would reach the mustanger as much as minutes after the wild horse did. Which means, he thought, that I'll be too late to keep him from being trampled to death. That horse, unless I miss my guess, means to put him out of commission once and for all. He rode on, sitting his saddle again, his eyes never leaving the wild horse, which did not slow its pace even slightly.

Neither did Sutton. He increased his speed and as he did so he thought he saw the mustanger move. But he knew he could have been wrong. It could have been merely the dust swirling around the man making it seem as if he had moved. Dead? Sutton wasn't sure if the mustanger was alive or not. He knew only that he had to try his best to keep him from going under the unshod hooves of the relentlessly oncoming wild horse.

He grabbed his lariat as he passed the downed man, heading straight for the wild horse. He stood up in his stirrups again and this time, as he swerved slightly to avoid colliding with the wild horse, brought the coiled rope down in a stunning blow that struck the head of the oncoming mustang, which reeked of rank sweat.

His blow brought a series of loud snorts from the animal. It also managed to slow the animal slightly. But the blow did not stop the mustang.

Sutton wheeled his horse and went racing after the one that had passed him. He quickly gained on it and this time, reluctantly, but knowing he had to do what he had made up his mind to do in order to save the downed mustanger, he drew his six-gun and fired.

The wild horse gave a ragged scream as blood flowed from its shattered skull. It halted, screamed weakly again, and then fell to the ground where it lay convulsing in its death throes.

Sutton drew rein, holstered his gun, and slid out of the saddle. He went running up to the mustanger who was now, he was relieved to see, propping himself up on his elbows and staring groggily into the dust surrounding him. When Sutton reached the man, he hauled him to his feet, put an arm around his waist, and began to lead him toward the black.

"I'll give you a boost up," he told the mustanger when they reached the black.

When the mustanger was in the saddle, Sutton climbed up in front of him and moved his horse out. He glanced back over his shoulder at the now lifeless horse he had shot. The sight of the animal brought the bitter bile of regret to his throat. But he knew he had done the right thing. Knew that if he had not done what he did the mustanger would be dead by now.

Behind him in the saddle, the man he had rescued mumbled something Sutton didn't catch although he did catch his companion's surly tone. Minutes later, as they rode double toward the mustanger's mount, which was quietly grazing some distance away, the man muttered, "Now see what you've done. Thanks to you, neither one of us has his hands on any of those horses."

"I wasn't intending to do you out of that herd," Sutton said sharply. "I was meaning to help you round them up."

The mustanger gave a skeptical snort. "Gone," he muttered mournfully. "Every last one of them."

Sutton successfully resisted the powerful impulse to elbow the man down to the ground and leave him far behind. He also resisted the even more powerful impulse to call the man a colorfully obscene name that was blazing unspoken in his mind.

"Mister," snarled the mustanger, "how come you

never learned to mind your own business and not try
to steal what was rightfully mine since I seen those
mustangs first?"

"Get yourself down out of my saddle," an exasper-
ated Sutton angrily ordered as he drew rein next to the
mustanger's mount. "I told you I wasn't after those
horses for myself. I was trying to help you catch
them."

"I'd as soon believe that as believe that fleas hate
hounds."

"Believe it or not, it's the truth. But I don't at all
fancy standing here trying to convince you of that fact.
I've things to do and lessons to learn. The first lesson
being how to mind my own business and the second
being to never so much as give the time of day, let
alone a helping hand, to a stranger such as yourself."

The mustanger climbed down out of the saddle and
stood somewhat unsteadily, his hands on his hips, as he
stared insolently up at Sutton.

He was a man who looked to Sutton to be about fifty
years old. As he studied him, Sutton thought that it
could very well be that it wasn't so much years that
showed on the man's face, but the ravages of wind and
weather and the rough life of a mustanger that had
taken their toll. He stood, Sutton estimated, about
midway between five and six feet. His legs were
slightly bowed, the mark of a man who had spent most
of his life looking at the world from between a horse's
ears. His body overall was wiry but his shoulders were
broad and his legs looked solid. His eyes were as blue
as a new pair of Frisco jeans, his broad nose bent, his
lips thin. His hair and bristling mustache were un-
kempt and clearly hadn't seen a scissor in weeks,
maybe even months.

"What are you, mister, a back-in-the-hills horse

breeder like me?" he asked Sutton. "Is that why you were trying to take those horses away from me?"

Sutton sighed. "I'm no horse breeder. When I spotted you, I saw you could use some help so I—"

"I never needed no help! I was doing fine on my own."

"The herd, it split in two. You couldn't have rounded up all of them. You would have lost half of them the way you were going."

"Not so! I could have got them all if only you hadn't of interfered."

"Well, you can set your mind at ease on that score. I'm through interfering with you, as you put it. In fact, I wish I'd never laid an eye on you, to tell you the gospel truth. Though if I hadn't that wild horse that came back after you would have turned you into a mud pie by now, sure as shooting he would have."

"That horse weren't no worry to me," the mustanger argued. "Why, I was just getting set to kick him in the snoot when you come riding by like you knew what you was doing only you didn't."

"*You* were getting set to kick *him* in the snoot?" Sutton laughed incredulously. "More like he was getting set to pound you down into the ground like a man would a post in a hole."

The mustanger's lips worked. His mustache quivered. His blue eyes glittered. "Maybe you're right. Maybe I did need a bit of help back there. When my horse, damn him, threw me, I think I landed on my head. At least right this minute my head feels like it's so big I couldn't crowd it into a corral. Not to mention all the bees that are still buzzing about inside it. Maybe I do owe you some kind of thanks after all."

"I'm not looking for thanks."

"What are you looking for?"

"A stallion called Wildfire."

The mustanger's eyes widened. He let out a shrill whistle. "So that's it, is it? You're out here hunting that tricky son of a bitch, are you? Well, I wish you luck on account of you'll be needing it just like any man foolhardy enough to go chasing after a will-o'-the-wisp needs more than his fair share of luck."

Sutton made no comment. He turned his horse and was about to ride away when the mustanger said, "Lots of men have tried to catch him. But that Wildfire, he won't let himself be caught. Too smart and far too stubborn for that he is. Even I couldn't catch that big fellow."

Sutton nodded. "After what I've seen today about how you go about chasing mustangs, I'm inclined to believe you on that count."

"Don't you go getting smart with me, mister. I'm your elder by more years than I care to count. Show some respect—or didn't they teach you such virtues wherever it is you hail from?"

Ignoring the mustanger's goading, Sutton moved out.

"My name's Buck," the mustanger called out to him. "Buck Hawthorn. What's yours?"

When Sutton didn't answer, Hawthorn scurried after him and got a grip on his bridle, halting the black. "Maybe the two of us got off on the wrong foot, mister," Hawthorn said. "But maybe we can make up and maybe be friends. I might be able to help you catch Wildfire if that's what you want to do."

Sutton looked down at Hawthorn. "How might you be able to help me catch Wildfire?"

"I know these mountains better than most men, if I do say so myself. Been horse hunting in these parts for the better part of ten years now. Not doing bad at the business neither, though I'm not one to brag. I've not seen you hereabouts before so I reckon I know this country a whole lot better than you do—"

"I've done my share of mustanging some years back down in Texas where I come from," Sutton interrupted. "I reckon I can manage on my own, thanks just the same."

"Well, now, don't that beat all!" Hawthorn exclaimed. "I had you figured at first for an outlaw of one stripe or another. You got that wary look in your eyes like outlaws have. But come to think on it that's the same kind of slick look most mustangers got in their eyes too."

"If you'll let go of my bridle, I'll be obliged to you, Hawthorn."

The mustanger maintained his hold on the bridle as he said, "I figure I owe you something. Not much— but something. For the way you saved my life—or at least one or two of my limbs—from that nasty bit of horseflesh back there. You're welcome to come along with me to my place. It's not much, just a little cabin hid back in the hills. But it's better than the great outdoors, especially when it rains. I could tell you all I know about Wildfire and about the land he likes to mosey around in. So what do you say, mister? By the way, you got a name, have you?"

"Name's Luke Sutton. And what I say is I'll ride along with you to your place and hear what you've got to say about Wildfire. I will, that is, if it don't turn out that all you've got to tell me is a passel of tall tales without a grain of truth in any single one of them."

"Now, whatever in the world would make you think, Luke, that I'm a tall-tale teller?"

"The way you claimed at first that you were set to kick that broomtail in the snoot when you knew as well as me that he was about to make mincemeat out of you."

Hawthorn assumed an expression of indignation for a moment, but it quickly collapsed into a smile and a snicker. "A man's got to do what he can to preserve some shred of dignity, now, don't he, Luke?"

"Not to mention a cantankerous disposition."

"Me? Cantankerous? You must have me mixed up with some other gent. But never mind about that now. Let's ride."

They did, and as they journeyed up the side of a steep mountain, making their way cautiously, their mounts' feet occasionally slipping on the stony terrain, Hawthorn informed Sutton that he would do well to watch his step in the area.

"Why?" Sutton asked.

"On account of these here hills is filled to overflowing with stud killers and other unsavory types like hide peelers, who'd as soon shoot you as look at you, especially so if you get in the way of their pleasure like you did with me today. That time you were lucky on account of I'm an understanding, not to mention tolerant, type of man. You might not be so lucky next time with all the trash that's loose in these hills like a veritable plague of locusts."

Sutton couldn't help himself; he smiled. What else, he asked himself with a philosophical shrug, was he to do. Hawthorn seemed determined to believe his own interpretation of what had happened earlier, and apparently nothing he could say would change the man's mind.

"Used to be," Hawthorn continued, "this was a peaceful place. But not anymore it's not. Everybody, it seems, is at everybody else's throat nowadays. They all seem set on getting what they want and everybody else be damned in their getting."

"You say you've been breeding horses up here in the hills," Sutton prompted.

"That I have, yes. But I don't just bring any stud and mare together to do their little dance, no sirree. I use judgement. And good sense. You won't catch me mating a fifteen-hundred-pound stud with a mare that tops the scales at only seven or eight hundred pounds, and then, what's worse, mating their offspring with some pony somewhere and then crossing back to, say, a draft stallion. Like I said, I use good sense and good judgement in my breeding."

"From the little I've seen of the wild herds so far," Sutton said, "it looks to me like there are a lot of blood-lines mixed up in these horses. I spotted what looked to me like some horses that stood tall enough to be Conestogas—or to have some Conestoga blood in them."

Hawthorn gave Sutton a shrewd look. "You know about Conestogas, do you?"

"Enough to know that a lot of them that were supposed to haul wagons and people across the plains to California, Oregon, and Washington got other notions in their heads, and escaped to pursue the free and easy life on their own. I know it was some German breeders back east who developed the line and that they wound up with good sturdy animals that stood as much as seventeen hands high."

"Out here we got some other types of horses too. Canadians from up above the border that drifted down this way over the years. Then there's the drafts from back in the States—Pennsylvania, to be exact about it. Not to mention the Indian ponies and good Spanish stock. A man sure needs a sharp eye if he's not to wind up with a no-account bunch of wild-and-woolies like the average mustang is.

"You got to have a real sharp eye in this business. You don't have one and you'll settle for any old cayuse you can get your rope on. That way's the road to ruin for a horse breeder. The horses that belonged a long time ago to the Cayuse Indians, they've gone downhill fast—and they weren't all that good to begin with. They mated here and they mated there when the urge was upon them, and the result is that a whole bunch of mustangs these days are nothing but undersized and scrawny crow-bait."

"What's the aim of your breeding program?"

"There ain't but just one. I breed horses for the plow, to pull wagons, and to take a saddle. It depends on what I've got to work with at any given time and who around here wants to buy what kind of horses. The farmers, they mostly want stock that'll work well in harness. But there's a fair share of folk who want saddle horses. It all works out in the wash as a rule. I'm usually able to sell folk what they want at any given time. If I can't, I can catch and break, like as not, what they want."

"I spotted Wildfire just before I ran into you," Sutton told Hawthorn. "That horse looks to me like he's got more than a little Spanish blood in him. I'd bet my best boots his ancestors came up out of Mexico to here. You can spot a horse with Spanish blood without too much trouble. A horse that has it's speedy and built nice and solid. His height though makes me think he's also part Conestoga. But it's his speed that stands out above all else. Maybe he's got a great-granddaddy or great-grandma that was an English running horse."

"He's a wonder, no doubt about that."

"You see much of him, do you?"

"Oh, I do, yes sirree. He lets himself be seen. It's like as if he doesn't care if you spot him. As if he's daring you to try to catch him."

"I had just met up with a woman named Judith Fletcher when I spotted him. It seems Miss Fletcher is dead set against anybody catching Wildfire. She deliberately stopped me from doing so. I was so mad I wanted to haul off and hit her."

"Did you?"

"Nope. I don't hit ladies."

"Had you hit her she would probably have gone running right to her daddy, and then old Abe Fletcher would have come a-hunting your hide."

"You know Miss Fletcher?"

"Her and her daddy both. He's a cattle rancher from around here."

The two men rode on past a waterfall that seemed to pour down from the sky. When they had passed it, Hawthorn pointed and said, "Down that slope and around that bend is where my cabin's at."

"It looks like a man could break his neck trying to get down there," Sutton observed as he eyed the steep slope that was pitted with holes in some places and covered with smooth sheets of limestone in others.

"He could," Hawthorn agreed cheerfully. "But if he don't he'll soon get used to going down and coming up that slope. So will his horse—if it don't break a leg and have to be shot. Point is prowlers tend to stay away from my place on account of how hard it is to get to. And with it being well out of the way as it is, there's not much reason for anybody passing through to risk his neck heading down there. Come on. I'll go first. We'll take it nice and slow, seeing as how this is your first time on the slope."

Sutton followed Hawthorn down the slope, leaning

back in the saddle, praying that his black wouldn't lose its footing. But the black, placing one foot carefully in front of the other and with its body slanted backward to compensate for the angle of the incline, made it to the bottom without incident.

Letting out the breath he hadn't realized he had been holding, Sutton rounded the bend with Hawthorn to find the man's cabin situated in a broad valley, with its rear wall set almost flush with the tall pines that served it as a windbreak. Beside it was a three-sided shed.

"Looks cozy," Sutton observed.

"I like it fine."

"Where do you keep your horses?"

"Come on. I'll show you."

Hawthorn and Sutton both dismounted and, after sheltering their horses in the shed, made their way through some woods until they came to a pole fence that barred the entrance to a wide box canyon. Beyond the fence milled scores of horses. To one side of the canyon were two pole corrals, one of which was empty and one of which held a lesser number of horses than did the canyon.

"Them's my Morgan mares," Hawthorn said, pointing to the horses in the corral. "I don't want them mixing in with those studs inside the canyon. That's one sure way to ruin a breeding program quicker'n a cat can claw you."

Later, in the cabin, Hawthorn hefted a sack full of what he informed Sutton was suet pudding. "It's swole up nice now," he declared. "I left it here to swell when I rode out this morning. It's not fancy food but it'll fill you. I put some raisins and dried currants in it. I'll make a dip of sugar water with a dollop of vanilla extract in it to put on it. But first I'll lay a fire—"

"I'll do it, Buck. Got to do something to earn my keep."

When Sutton had a fire blazing in the hearth, Hawthorn hung a pot over it and, when the water in the pot was boiling, he dropped the sack of suet pudding into it and covered it. While the pudding was boiling, he kneaded a mixture of flour, water, and sugar, and from this made miniature griddle cakes; these he dropped in a greased skillet which he then held over the fire.

When the two men had finished their meal and Sutton was drinking a second cup of coffee, Hawthorn said, "You spoke before about earning your keep. How are you at roughing out broncs?"

"I can hold my own. Bronc stomping was my trade for years, like I told you."

"Then we'll go out tomorrow and try to catch ourselves some mustangs. Then, with the two of us to rough them out, the work will go a lot faster. What we'll do is we'll head out to Wildfire's home range. What do you say to that, Luke?"

"That suits me fine. Maybe this time, should I sight Wildfire, I'll be able to get my loop on him—unless Miss Fletcher should appear on the scene and do me like she did the last time we met."

"Don't get your hopes of catching Wildfire up too high. Even without Judith Fletcher to put a crimp in your style, you'll have your hands full—the both of us together would—getting a rope on that slick stud."

Next morning, just after dawn, Sutton and Hawthorn left the cabin and rode out, driving two tame Morgan mares ahead of them. Hawthorn's mount was trailing a travois on which was fastened a thick pile of canvas and a number of juniper poles.

"There's a water hole about six, seven miles due

north of here," Hawthorn informed Sutton. "Wildfire appears to be partial to it. Or maybe the white mare that leads his herd is. Anyway, we can try our luck there."

When they reached the water hole, they discovered there was no sign of Wildfire or, for that matter, any other wild horse.

"We'll set up our corral around the water hole," Hawthorn said. "The horses usually follow that ridge up there on their way here. Being high up on it gives them the chance to scout for any danger that might be in the area. If there's none, they come down here and head straight for the water."

"I've never known anybody to set up a canvas corral before," Sutton said as he helped Hawthorn unload the travois and then removed the travois from Hawthorn's horse. "You sure it'll hold any horses we get inside it?"

Hawthorn chuckled. "The canvas corral—that's my own idea and a bright one it is, if I do so say myself. It outfoxes mustangs. They think the canvas is a solid wall so they don't try to bust through it. Oh, once in a while one of them will get over the top of it and go back to being free but the same thing happens with a willow or a wire corral. Here, take this hammer and pound some of those juniper stakes in a circle around the water hole while I unlimber the canvas."

Sutton took the hammer from Hawthorn and proceeded to pound stakes into the ground at intervals around the water hole, after which he helped Hawthorn stretch the canvas, which was a good eight feet tall, around the perimeter of the stakes. Then the two men led the two tame Morgan mares into the corral they had made, and fashioned a gate which they left wide open.

"Now all we got to do is wait," Hawthorn announced when they had finished. "We'll dig us some nests. Make yourself one on that side of the gate. I'll make mine over on this side."

Using a shovel Hawthorn had brought with him, they dug holes in the ground deep enough to hide in. After getting down into the holes and covering themselves with brush, they waited.

Less than an hour later, Sutton heard the faint pounding of hooves in the distance. Peering through the brush covering him, he watched the top of the ridge. He was rewarded a few minutes later by the sight of a small herd of horses following the ridge line. But he was disappointed to see no sign of Wildfire among the mustangs.

Suddenly, as if in response to a signal, the herd halted. They stood almost motionless on the ridge, one or more of them moving slightly from time to time, but none of them venturing down from the ridge. Then, a mare turned and vanished from sight on the far side of the ridge. The other horses promptly wheeled and followed her until they were all gone, the sound of their hoofbeats fading fast.

Hawthorn threw aside the brush covering him and climbed out of his hole.

"The corral spooked them," Sutton stated as he joined Hawthorn, who was staring up at the empty ridge.

"I'd hoped they would've come down to investigate," Hawthorn said. "Then after a while I figured they'd move inside the corral with my two mares there. But they, it seems, had other ideas. They've no doubt gone to Pole Creek, which is about two miles east of here."

"We're going after them?"

Hawthorn shook his head. "By the time we got there they'd have drunk their fill and gone. No, what we'll do is take it easy here for the rest of the day till near dusk when they'll be wanting water again."

"What then?"

"Before dusk comes, I'll ride over to Pole Creek and if they show up there tonight, I'll run them off. They'll be thirsty enough by that time to come back here where you'll be waiting for them. I'll be right behind them but not near enough so they can see me following them. If any of them go inside the corral here, you just jump up out of your nest and get the gate in place and secure it before they know what's happening. Mind you, you'll have to act fast as fire in sawdust. You don't—you let one of those broomtails get his wits about him and he'll come crashing through the gate before you can get it closed and stomp you to death. Of course, you don't have to mess with this matter at all if you don't want to. I won't fault you for backing out. It's damn dangerous work."

"I know it is. I'll do my part."

"So be it then."

That evening, as shadows began to lengthen and the first of the coming night's prowling coyotes howled, Sutton was crouched in his hole next to the open gate. He listened but heard nothing other than the coyote. He had about given up hope that any mustangs would appear when a familiar rumbling came to his ears and he knew that some horses were on their way.

When he caught sight of them up on the ridge, he recognized them as the same herd that had come to the water hole that morning. He crouched down in his hole to wait.

As the sky above him turned a bright orange, as if

burning up in the last rays of the sun, which was below the horizon, a mare started slowly down from the
ridge. When she reached level ground, she swung her
head around and the herd that was still on the ridge
began moving down toward her. Forming a herd once
again a few minutes later, the horses moved cautiously
toward the corral enclosing the water hole and the two
Morgan mares.

Sutton, barely breathing, waited tensely as the orange sky turned blood red.

The herd slowly circled the corral. Then they circled it a second time. Something suddenly spooked
them, something Sutton had neither seen nor heard,
causing them to flee halfway up the slope that led to
the ridge.

But some time later, they returned to circle the canvas corral. A mare was the first one to enter it. She had
no sooner done so than she swiftly turned and galloped back out of it again. She stood snorting and
prancing nervously, warily watching as two colts entered the corral side by side.

Sutton heard the sounds the colts made as they began to drink. The other horses moved tentatively toward the corral entrance. A half-grown stallion went
inside. Finally, the remainder of the herd entered the
corral. They had no sooner done so than Sutton was
up on his feet and slamming shut the gate of the corral.
He quickly secured it and as quickly fled the area, in
case Hawthorn had been wrong and the horses
trapped inside the corral decided to knock it down in
order to escape.

They did not.

He could hear them moving about inside the enclosure but the canvas did not so much as flutter from the
touch of a horse's body. This indicated that the ani-

mals were staying well away from what they apparently perceived as a solid wall, just as Hawthorn had said they would do.

The polestar was gleaming in the dark sky when Hawthorn crested the ridge and rode down to rejoin Sutton.

"Well, Luke, we got them!" he crowed. "Come morning, we'll take the whole bunch back home with us."

FIVE

EARLY THE NEXT MORNING, after a breakfast of jerky washed down with water, Sutton and Hawthorn proceeded to prepare the horses they had captured for the trip back to Hawthorn's cabin.

They worked as a team. Hawthorn, mounted, would rope one of the horses, and his own horse would keep the rope taut as Sutton moved in on the tethered animal. When he reached it, he used his bowie knife to cut a ligament in one of the horse's front legs, allowing fluid to drain from the wound; this would, in a very short time, cause the leg to stiffen, thus preventing the horse from running until the wound healed.

Later, at Hawthorn's suggestion, they switched roles. Sutton roped and threw one of the mustangs. Hawthorn then stuffed the animal's nostrils with grass and sewed them closed with a sack needle and coarse thread he had brought with him, saying as he did so, "If he can't get his breath, he won't run."

Such proved to be the case later when both men drove the herd out of the corral. All the horses—those whose legs Sutton had cut and those whose nostrils had been sewn up by Hawthorn—tried to escape, found they could not run without great distress because of what the two mustangers had done to them, and so quickly settled down into a trot and then a resigned walk with both mounted men flanking them.

Led by the Morgan mares, they made a slow and

generally uneventful journey, with the single exception of one mare who would not give up trying to escape. The horse would leave the herd, run a short distance, blow through its mouth because of its sewn-up nostrils, and then try to run again.

Sutton would ride out after her and turn her back into the herd, where she would remain for a short time before repeating her performance.

The journey ended at Hawthorn's cabin a little after noon. There Sutton and Hawthorn turned their captured horses into the canyon corral where Sutton moved cautiously among them, cutting the threads that bound their nostrils and removing the grass that clogged them so they could breathe normally again.

Once outside the canyon again with its gate closed, he stood beside Hawthorn who was studying the captured horses.

Hawthorn pointed at a wooly-hided buckskin that had a wild look in its eye; it bared its teeth over and over again as if challenging an invisible enemy. "That one's a thousand pounds of hell on the hoof," he remarked, his tone a blend of awe and admiration. "He won't take kindly to being busted but it's got to be done."

"I'll do it," Sutton volunteered, his eyes on the buckskin, whose mane was a tangled mass of hair and cockleburs. "Unless you've set your sights on roughing him out yourself."

Hawthorn gave Sutton a sidelong glance. Cocking an eyebrow, he said, "You think you're equal to that one, do you?"

"Maybe a little better than equal. Maybe not. There's but one way to find out, isn't there?"

Hawthorn was silent for a moment as he studied Sutton. Then: "Son, you remind me of myself when I was your age. Back then there wasn't nothing or no one, including old Nick himself, who could stop me from doing whatever it was I felt like doing. Oh, I had sand in those days, let me tell you. And you—you're the selfsame way, it seems. For me, looking at you's a little like looking in a mirror at myself. You're just as foolhardy as I was when I was as young as you."

"Buck, the way you talk a man can't be sure whether he's just gotten a compliment or a tongue-lashing. But be that as it may, I'll go rough out that buckskin now if you've no objections."

"I've none, Luke. But mind you—be careful. Look at him. He's as mean-looking as a mountain about to fall on you. And he's a fighter too."

"A veteran for sure," Sutton agreed as he noted the patches of white hair on the horse's hide, which had grown in over deep wounds that had probably been inflicted by another stallion. "You can read his fighting history on his hide as sure as you can tell where a cowhide's been by the brands it bears."

"I've got a kak and a hackamore in the cabin you can use," Hawthorn said. "I'll go get 'em."

While Hawthorn was gone, Sutton mounted his black and rode into the corral where he roped the big buckskin; then he dragged it, bucking and pawing the ground, out of the corral. He leaned down and closed the corral gate and roped the buckskin over to the empty pole corral. Once he had the horse inside it, he removed his rope from the animal's neck, rode out of the corral, and dismounted.

Hawthorn returned a few minutes later and handed him the blanket, bronc saddle, and hackamore he had retrieved from the cabin. "That there's a good saddle," he said. "It's three-quarter rigged and slick-forked. It'll serve you well."

Sutton carried the gear and the rope he had removed from the buckskin's neck into the corral. The wild horse snorted nervously and began to circle. Sutton kept turning so that he was always facing the animal, as he shook out a long loop. He watched the stallion as he swung the loop he had made and, when he saw his chance, he threw his rope and succeeded in forefooting the horse. He jerked in the slack, his booted heels dug deep in the ground, the rope anchored across his hip. He timed his pull carefully. When he made it, the buckskin's front feet flew out from under him.

The horse crashed to the ground, still snorting, strings of slimy saliva flying from between open lips which revealed thick white teeth.

Sutton moved in on the downed horse, flipped two half hitches over the loop on the animal's front feet; then, with the front feet secured, he flipped another half hitch over both hind feet, drawing them up to the front feet. One more quick half hitch and he had the buckskin where he wanted him—on the ground with all four of his feet tied so that he was unable to get up.

But there was one problem. When the horse had hit the ground it had done so on its left side and Sutton wanted—needed—him on his right side. He solved the problem by gripping the pigging ropes with both hands and rolling the buckskin over on his right side.

He picked up the hackamore Hawthorn had given him and placed it over the horse's head. Then he placed the blanket and then the saddle on the animal. Gripping the pigging ropes again, he moved the horse's body slightly and then, getting down on one knee, he slid his hand under the horse's hot body until he could grasp the saddle's cinch ring. When he had it in his hand, he drew it forward under the animal's body and then proceeded to fasten the saddle to the buckskin's back.

Rising, he signaled to Hawthorn who opened the corral gate. Then he crouched, getting ready to step into the saddle, as he removed the loops from the horse's feet. As the ropes came off, the buckskin struggled to its feet. At the same time, Sutton swung into the saddle. When the buckskin was up, it found itself with a man on its back.

It bucked.

It sunfished.

Sutton held tightly to the hackamore as the horse made four lightning-fast leaps in a row, whirled, and then stood suddenly stiff-legged. He barely had time to brace himself before the mustang stood first on his heels and then on his head, his body flying up into the air and then down again with a spine-cracking jolt that almost unsaddled Sutton.

Hawthorn, standing outside the corral, whooped with glee, slapped his hat against his thigh, and yelled, "He's a beast with a bellyful of bedsprings, Luke. Hold on tight or he'll send you to heaven before your time!"

Sutton held on with both hands, his body snapping back and forth and then whipsawing from side to side as the mustang under him humped its back, shot straight up into the air, came down, and shook itself vigorously several times in a futile effort to unseat its rider.

Sutton's legs flapped like wings against the side of the horse. He coughed as dust raised by the animal's bucking invaded his nostrils.

Unexpectedly, the buckskin stood still.

Sutton, suspicious of what the animal had in mind, gripped it with his knees and tightened his grip on the hackamore.

The mustang bucked again, its body bent double as it flew almost four feet up into the air. Sutton's body rose from the saddle and, when he came down, he just barely missed hitting the saddle horn. Up on his hind legs went the mustang. Sutton, to keep from sliding backward out of the saddle, seized the animal's neck with his left arm and held on as tightly as he could.

Down came the mustang's front legs with a bone-snapping crack.

"Hang on, Luke!" Hawthorn yelled, a note of apprehension now in his voice. "That critter's out to stomp you into the ground so deep you'll take roots and sprout!"

The buckskin raced out of the corral, its hooves pounding the ground.

Sutton let go of the animal's neck and held on to the hackamore with both hands while simultaneously gripping the buckskin's barrel with both legs in an effort to remain in the saddle. The mustang had gone only a short distance when, as it ran, it began to shake its huge body from side to side, trying to dislodge Sutton.

Cold sweat streamed down Sutton's back and chest. It slicked his face and ran into his eyes, temporarily blinding him.

The buckskin suddenly came to a skidding, dust-stirring halt. It threw its hind legs into the air as if it were taking a kick at the sky. Balancing on its front feet, it kicked a second time. Then it again leaped straight up into the air several times in succession. Each time it had gone as high as it could it would vigorously shake itself, causing Sutton to wonder whether the cinch would hold.

It did.

Hawthorn hooted happily outside the corral.

"You've damn near nailed him, Luke! But that last time—he threw you so high it's a wonder you ain't got birds nesting in your hair!"

Hawthorn's laughter faded as the buckskin began to run again with Sutton holding on with both hands and both legs. When, to his dismay, he felt the saddle begin to slide beneath him, he considered making a leap from the horse's back—if it ever slowed down for so much as a second—to keep himself from being thrown in case the saddle should slide all the way down under the horse's barrel. But then the fight suddenly went out of the mustang. It came to a shuddering halt and stood with its head hanging down, breathing heavily, seemingly unmindful of the way its long tangled mane covered its eyes.

Sutton sat the saddle waiting for the animal's next move, unwilling to believe that the ordeal was over, that the fuzztail had finally given up. When the horse moved forward a few steps, he stiffened, expecting more sunfishing, more bucking. None came. The mustang halted. Stood with its head still lowered. Took a few more steps. Shuddered. Swung its head around to eye Sutton balefully.

He put his heels to it and headed back toward the corral. Still expecting more angry resistance, he was surprised but pleased when the buckskin covered the ground meekly and without trying to fight him. When they reached the corral, Hawthorn was waiting for them, his eyes alight, a smile on his face.

He greeted Sutton with, "That horse, he sure is frolicsome, ain't he?"

"Frolicsome's not exactly the word I'd use to describe him," Sutton responded. "Murdering's more like it," he added as he stepped down from the saddle.

"Watch it, Luke!"

But Sutton had seen the buckskin bare its teeth so he was prepared for the horse's attempt to bite him. He hit it on the side of its head with his fist, and knew by the cowed reaction of the once-wild horse that the battle was finally over and he had won it.

"Judging by that performance you just put on," Hawthorn said, "you must have been hell among the yearlings when you were a mustanger down in Texas."

"I did alright," Sutton said modestly and added, "You plan to break that whole bunch we brought in?"

"I do," Hawthorn replied. "And since you got us off to such a good start I see no point in quitting now, do you?"

For the rest of the day the two men worked together breaking the rest of the wild horses they had captured. By the time they were finished, more than an hour after the sun had set, Sutton was painfully aware of muscles and tendons and ligaments in his body that he had not been conscious of since his earlier days as a bronc peeler. But his severe aches and pains did not keep him from eating two hearty portions of the meal Hawthorn cooked for them, nor did they keep him from sleeping soundly throughout the night.

After breakfast the following morning, Hawthorn announced that he was going to check the stock they had roughed out the day before to make sure the horses would submit to saddling and riding. He invited Sutton to join him in the task.

"If it's all the same to you, Buck, I'd like to go see if I can't run down Wildfire."

"Go to it, son, and good luck to you."

Sutton rode out a few minutes later, heading for the water hole where he had helped Hawthorn capture the wild horses the day before. He was nearing it when he heard the sound of rifle fire in the distance. He went galloping toward the sound, fearful that someone might already have found—and perhaps killed—Wildfire.

As he rounded a bend and the water hole came into sight, he saw four men up ahead of him. Two of them were on a slight rise to the west of the water hole. One was perched in a sycamore behind the canvas corral that surrounded the water hole. The fourth man, who was older than the other three, was mounted and sitting his saddle with a rifle in his hands due east of the entrance to the corral, which, Sutton noted, had its gate closed.

Inside the corral, he saw six mustangs, two of them lying dead on the ground. He was relieved to discover that none of the horses was Wildfire.

He rode up to the older man who suddenly stood up in his stirrups, raised his rifle, took aim, and fired a round over the top of the canvas wall. The bullet struck one of the four mustangs which were milling nervously about inside the corral.

A smile wrinkled the rough features of the older man's face. His brown eyes gleamed. He reached up, tilted his sweat-stained Stetson back on his head, and resumed his seat.

"Howdy," Sutton greeted him. "Are you fellows stud killers?"

"Not if you mean are me and my three hands hired like some men are to kill mustangs for a fee per head," the older man answered, rising up in his stirrups again and squeezing off another round, which missed its target. "But we're here, as is plain to see, to kill those fuzztails we've got trapped inside that corral.

"Did you ever in your born days see such a contraption? I don't know how or why it holds horses but hold them it most decidedly does. Why it's made out of *canvas*, for Christ's sweet sake!"

"I helped build it," Sutton volunteered. "My name's Luke Sutton."

The older man, back in his saddle again, lowered his rifle. He gave Sutton an appraising glance and then offered his hand. "I'm Mel Dunbar."

As the two men shook hands, Dunbar continued, "I run some five hundred head of cattle on my range east of here. You say you built that crazy corral?"

"Helped build it. I'm partnering temporarily with a mustanger name of Buck Hawthorn."

"I know Buck. I reckon everybody around here knows that old goat. He's as cantankerous as they come. But good with horses. I've bought more than a few from him in my time. Was that canvas corral Buck's idea perchance?"

Sutton nodded. "Buck says he figures the fuzztails think the canvas is a solid wall so they don't try to bust through it. He might be right. All I know is it works."

"Me and my hands—those three fellows scattered around the water hole—we came upon those six wild horses inside that corral when we rode up. It was a simple-as-pie matter to shut the gate and then start shooting them like fish in a barrel."

"You've no love for mustangs, I take it."

"None whatsoever. Wild horses are the bane of my existence, not to mention being as bad as blizzards for the cattle business. They ruin the range and kill stock by stampeding a herd. I don't take any particular pleasure in killing them, but a man's got to protect his interests and my interests happen to be cattle and the rangeland they need to thrive on."

Another shot sounded. A horse inside the corral

went down to thrash about on the ground for several minutes before dying.

Dunbar stood up in his stirrups and fired again. This time he hit the horse he had been aiming at. It leaped up into the air and then came down to stand unsteadily on all four wavering legs. It shuddered and shook before its front legs buckled and it went down on its knees, then rolled over on its side on the ground.

"I've not seen you in these parts before, Sutton," Dunbar commented. "Are you a stud killer?"

"Nope. I'm here to try to catch a stallion folks call Wildfire."

"You don't say?"

"I'm teamed up temporarily like I said before with Buck Hawthorn until I can get my rope on Wildfire. I'm being paid to catch him and bring him to a man who's waiting on me back in Virginia City. Are those horses in the corral part of his herd?"

"Don't know but I doubt it. There was no sign of Wildfire when we got here and he doesn't as a rule let part of his herd stray like those six must have done from somewhere."

"Then you've seen no sign of him around here?"

"None. And if I ever see him again it'll be too soon. Him and his herd roaming on my range are worse than rabbits in a cabbage patch."

"I've heard ranchers claim that one horse will eat as much grass as two cows."

"That's true as the Good Book's word," Dunbar said. "Not to mention how they crush the grass with their sharp hooves and eat what they don't kill down closer to the ground than do sheep, which are real close-croppers."

More shots rang out and Sutton watched the last of the wild horses inside the corral drop and die.

Dunbar said, "I can't tell you how many times that goddamn Wildfire and his herd have stampeded my cattle. I'd as soon kill that critter as look at him."

"Mr. Dunbar, I know you don't owe me anything but I'd like to ask a favor of you."

Dunbar waited, his steady gaze on Sutton.

"I'd be mighty obliged to you if you wouldn't, should you and your boys run into Wildfire, shoot him. If you'll just not do that and give me a little time to hunt him down, I'll have him out of your hair before long and for good."

Dunbar stroked his chin, his eyes still on Sutton. "I don't know that I can make you that kind of promise. As a matter of fact, I know I can't. That damned Wildfire and his herd have caused me more trouble and ruined more of my range and killed more of my cows in stampedes and put more holes in my water troughs and eaten more of the salt I put out for my stock than any other six herds of wild horses roaming about in these parts. No, sir, I just can't see my way clear to promise you not to shoot that devil should I see him. But maybe you'll get lucky and catch him before him and me cross paths again."

"Nice talking to you, Dunbar," a disappointed Sutton said. "Sorry we couldn't strike a bargain."

"Like I said though, you could get lucky and catch Wildfire before I can kill him."

Sutton turned his horse and rode away. He made his way back to where he had encountered Judith Fletcher —to the place she had referred to as part of Wildfire's home range. When he reached it, he rode it in ever-widening circles as he searched for sign of the stallion and his herd. He made his nooning in the shade of a locust tree, eating the biscuits and canned peaches he had brought with him from Hawthorn's cabin. It was

while he was finishing the last of the peaches and de-
vouring the remains of a rock-hard biscuit—made
barely edible by having been soaked in the sugary
syrup the peaches had been packed in—that he heard
the sound of pounding hooves in the distance.

Casting away what remained of his dinner, he
leaped to his feet and sprang into the saddle so quickly
that he startled his black, which ran aimlessly for a few
yards before he got the animal under control. When he
was sure from which direction the sound of running
horses was coming, he turned the black and headed
that way.

He had just topped a hummock that stretched for
more than a mile in either direction when he saw them
—Wildfire and his herd of mares and their foals. Good
thing, he thought, that horses have such a strong sense
of territory. He rode down from the hummock, heading for the herd. If they didn't, I'd have a whole lot
harder time running this bunch down.

He swerved and rode in on the herd from the rear.
No use handing Wildfire my calling card, he thought.
Not till I'm ready to and I'm not ready to, not yet, I'm
not. He caught up with the herd a few minutes later.
Using his coiled rope which he had taken from his
saddle horn, he drove several mares from the herd. As
they veered off at a right angle to avoid the flailing
rope, Sutton moved in on the mares that were now at
the rear of the herd. He struck the nearest one with his
rope and then the one directly in front of it. As several
mares peeled away from the main herd, he closed in on
those now at the rear and drove several more away.
When he had thinned the herd to his satisfaction, he
dropped back, rode to the left, turned the black, and
then headed back to the herd, moving in on it from a

sharp angle. His goal—to cut Wildfire off from what remained of his herd.

As he neared the mustangs, several weaker colts dropped out of the running. Minutes later, a mare dropped her tail and quit the race.

Sutton let out a loud yell that careened across the shallow valley through which he and the herd were traveling. Wildfire, in response to the cry, swung his head around. When he saw Sutton, he abruptly put on a new burst of speed, obviously intending to outrun his pursuer.

The stud's maneuver suited Sutton fine. It left a gap between Wildfire and the nearest of the remainder of the herd still racing behind him. He moved into that gap. Then, turning around in the saddle, he whipped the noses of the mares and foals nearest to him with his rope, forcing them to fall back even further. Leaving them all behind, he turned his attention to Wildfire. The stud, seeing himself cut off from his herd, tried to turn and double back. But Sutton prevented him from doing so.

He fashioned a loop as he rode on in pursuit of Wildfire, whose body was now covered with a sweaty white foam. He was swinging his loop above his head and still riding hard and directly behind Wildfire when a rifle shot roared through the valley.

Wildfire's gait turned abruptly ragged and the white foam on his neck turned first pink and then red.

Sutton swore. Giving up the chase, he sharply turned his horse and headed west toward the gunman he had spotted standing at the edge of a grove of oak trees about fifty yards away.

He waved frantically to the rifleman and shouted to him in an attempt to stop him from killing Wildfire. Behind him, the stud and his herd continued to flee through the valley. Sutton glanced over his shoulder, hoping that the herd was out of the gunman's range by now, but he was disappointed to find that they were not. He deliberately placed himself and his horse directly in the rifleman's line of fire. He stood up in his stirrups and continued waving and yelling in an effort to deter the man from any further shooting.

He resumed his seat and his swearing as the gunman raised his rifle and again took aim. Pulling his Winchester from the saddle boot, Sutton brought it up and swiftly squeezed off a shot, deliberately aiming to the right of the man up ahead of him. His warning shot caused the man with the rifle to aim his weapon directly at Sutton.

As the rifleman squeezed off a round, Sutton ducked down and pressed his cheek against the neck of his horse. He heard the round whine harmlessly over his head. Then, less than a minute later, he was drawing rein and his horse was coming to a rough and dust-stirring stop only a few feet away from the rifleman.

"What the hell do you think I am?" Sutton roared at the man, leveling the barrel of his Winchester at him. "A mustang?"

"Save your breath to cool your coffee, mister," the rifleman shot back. "You shot at me. I shot back. Now get out of my way before I let light through you."

Sutton sprang from the saddle and, using his rifle as a club, knocked the gun from the other man's hands. As the man made a grab for his fallen weapon, Sutton gave him a hard jab with his rifle barrel, unbalancing him and sending him down to the ground. As the man started to rise, Sutton said, "Stay put if you know what's good for you." He glanced over his shoulder and was both relieved and disappointed to find that Wildfire and his herd had vanished.

"What right have you—" began the downed man.

Sutton interrupted him with, "I tried to get you to stop shooting by yelling at you. I waved to get your attention. But you paid me no mind at all. That round I fired wasn't meant to kill or even wound you. It went wide of you on purpose. I only fired it to get you to stop shooting."

"What right have you got to try to stop me from shooting?"

"That stud you shot—I want him. And I want him alive."

"He's not branded stock. You don't own him any-more than anybody else does. So you got no right to stop me from killing him."

Sutton said nothing for a moment as he studied the man who was still lying on the ground. He had a nar-row forehead and sunken cheeks. His eyes might have been dark blue or even black, but it was difficult to tell for sure because of the way his wide hat brim shaded his face. His nose looked as if it had been broken and there was a knife scar on his neck. He was stockily built, his body bearing more fat than muscle.

"You heard what I just said, mister," he prodded. "I said you got no right to stop me from killing any un-branded horse I come upon out here. And that stallion was not only unbranded, he was *wild*."

"What's your reason for wanting to kill him?" Sut-ton asked as he stepped back to allow the man to get to his feet.

The man did so. He slapped dust from his clothes with his hat, picked up his rifle, and stood facing Sut-ton. "I've got two good reasons for killing Wildfire," he said. "The first one is that I've been hired to kill as many wild horses as I can for a fee per head. I kill them, cut off their ears to prove I did kill them, and collect my money. The second reason is I just want to prove to myself I can do it, since nobody else has been able to stop his clock."

"Maybe you and me, we can work something out," Sutton suggested.

"What have you got in mind?" the rifleman inquired suspiciously.

"How much do you get paid for each kill you make? By the way, my name's Luke Sutton. What's yours?"

"I'm called Stoner and I get paid eight dollars cash money for every broomtail I kill."

"How would it be were I to pay you eight dollars right here and now and we call it the fee you would have got from whoever hired you for killing Wildfire."

Stoner began to smile but his expression was oddly joyless. "I could take your money and still kill Wildfire —or hadn't you thought of that, Sutton?"

"Oh, I'd thought of it alright. But I'm a man of my word and I thought maybe you are too."

"No deal."

"You mind my asking why not?"

"No, I don't mind. You see, what it is, I got another reason beyond the first two I already gave you for wanting to kill that stud. I got a grudge against him. I ran into him a few days ago. I shot a few of his mares —some of his foals too. Well, it would appear that he didn't take too kindly to that. So what did he do? He turned the rest of his herd and he sent them straight for me with him bringing up the rear where he'd be safe and sound. I tried shooting to turn them. They tried to turn only he wouldn't let them. The minute they'd try to get out of my line of fire, he'd be at them a-snapping and a-biting something all-fired fierce. Anyways, the end of it all was that I had to hightail it to hell away as fast as I could go else I'd've been trampled to death. I've been stalking him ever since and today I finally found him. He'd have been as dead as last summer's roses if you hadn't've come along."

"I'll double your price. I'll pay you sixteen dollars to leave him be."

"No dice," Stoner said, shaking his head. "Mr. Fletcher, he wouldn't like it if he found out I was shirking my duty. Why, he might even take it into his head to get rid of me and go hire himself some other stud killer to do the job he wants done so bad. Then where'd I be?"

Sutton turned and went to his black. Booting his rifle, he swung into the saddle. He was just about to ride away, convinced that there was no point in trying to bargain any further with Stoner but already thinking of another way to keep the man from killing Wildfire, when the stud killer smirked and said, "I wouldn't, were I you, try anything like that foolishness you did here today should you and me ever meet up again. Next time, you might not come out of it alive."

"Next time—if there is one," Sutton said flatly, "neither might you come out of such a meeting alive, Stoner. Now that's something that bears thinking on."

"Don't it, though? So I trust you'll give the matter the thought you yourself say it deserves."

Sutton moved his horse out, riding at an angle, his right hand on the butt of his revolver as he kept Stoner in sight, in case the stud killer should decide that now was the time to make his move.

But he didn't make a move and Sutton soon left him far behind.

SIX

AFTER LEAVING STONER and searching the area for the better part of an hour, finding no trace of Wildfire and his herd, Sutton returned to Hawthorn's cabin where he asked the mustanger where Abe Fletcher's cattle ranch was located.

Hawthorn told him and then asked, "You've got business with Fletcher, have you?"

"I have," Sutton answered. "I ran into a man today who works for Fletcher. A man named Stoner."

"I know most of Fletcher's hands. Never heard of one called Stoner."

"He's a new man and not your regular ranch hand. Stoner's a stud killer."

"Fletcher has hired himself one of that breed?" Hawthorn asked with undisguised surprise. "I knew he had been having wild horse trouble but Fletcher never struck me as a man who'd put a stud killer on his payroll. Maybe things have got so bad for him he figured he had no other choice. Still, it's a surprise to me. Fletcher always was a live-and-let-live sort of fellow."

"Be seeing you, Buck," Sutton said and started for the door.

"Hold on a minute," Hawthorn called out to him. When Sutton turned back to face him, he said, "I know it's not none of my business but what are you going to see Fletcher about? I ask on account of you've got a real mean look in your eyes and I hope you're not heading for trouble."

"I found Wildfire when I was out riding his home range today," Sutton said tonelessly. "I was running him and was just about to drop my loop on him when Stoner all of a sudden showed up and started shooting at him. Not at any of the horses in his herd—just at Wildfire himself. He shot him in the neck."

"Wildfire's dead?"

"He wasn't the last time I saw him. But I don't know how bad he was hurt. I saw blood but he was all sweated up so it was hard to tell what kind of a wound he had. Anyway, I had to let him go while I tried to stop Stoner from killing him."

"What happened?"

"I put a crimp in Stoner's style. But not, I reckon, for long. I offered to pay him the bounty he'd have got from Fletcher if he'd killed Wildfire—offered, as a matter of fact, to double it. He wouldn't hear of it. He told me he's got a grudge against Wildfire on account of how the horse almost killed him one time when he was hunting it. Seems he's bound and determined now to even the score by killing Wildfire."

"I think I can make out the lay of the land now," Hawthorn observed. "You're going to try to get Fletcher to call off his hired gun, is that it?"

"That's it exactly."

By the time Sutton reached the Fletcher spread later that day, the sun was low in the sky. He rode up to the long single-story ranch house and dismounted. After tethering his black to the hitch-rail in front of the house, he knocked on the heavy wooden door. It was opened by Judith Fletcher who could not disguise her surprise at the sight of Sutton.

"Good day to you, Miss Fletcher." He touched the brim of his hat to her.

"A good day to you too, Mr. Sutton—it is Mr. Sutton, isn't it? I do have the name right?"

"You do. I'm kind of surprised you remember it—and me—since we met just that one time and not under the most favorable conditions."

"Oh, I remember you—our meeting."

Sutton thought Judith blushed but he wasn't sure. She was wearing a yellow day dress eyeletted with brown velvet ribbons at the wrists, neck, and hemline. Its full skirt emphasized her shapely hips, and the lace trimming at her bodice was both pert and provocative.

"Won't you come in, Mr. Sutton?"

"Thank you." Sutton took off his hat and stepped inside a dim hall that was pleasantly cool. Judith led him to a parlor on one side of the house, where he waited until she had taken a seat before sitting down himself.

Then, facing her, he said, "I've come to have a talk with your father. Is he to home?"

"Yes, he is. He's out back either in the barn or the bunkhouse, I'm not sure. I'll go and get him for you."

Sutton rose as Judith did and said, "I don't want to disturb him. If he's busy, I could come back some other time."

"I don't think that will be necessary. Please wait a moment, Mr. Sutton."

When Judith had left the room, Sutton sat on the edge of his chair, twisting his hat in his hands and surveying the well-furnished room, which contained numerous pieces of heavy claw-footed furniture, a spinet, and a fireplace flanked by walls lined with shelves full of books.

He rose and went over to the shelves, scanning the

titles stacked upon them—Virgil, Dante, Dickens, and Shelley among them. He took down a copy of Chaucer's *Canterbury Tales* and was looking through it when his eye was caught by a passage from the Miller's Tale:

What! Absalom! For Jesus Christ's sweet tree,
Why are you up so early? Ben'cite!
What ails you now, man? Some gay girl, God knows,
Has brought you on the jump to my bellows:
By Saint Neot, you know well what I mean.

Some of the words echoed in his mind: *"What ails you now, man? Some gay girl . . ."*

An image of Judith Fletcher burned in his mind, lovely as the wondrous light of a bright summer's day. He saw her blue eyes blazing, an invitation in them. He saw her long auburn hair shining and shifting like a luminous sea with her every movement. He saw her slender hands, her full figure . . .

No doubt about it. Judith Fletcher was a very attractive woman. There was also no doubt about the fact that he had been glad to see her again. He was almost grateful to the stud killer, Stoner, whose attempt to kill Wildfire had brought him here to meet Judith Fletcher once again. No matter that he and she held opposing views on the matter of Wildfire's fate. What mattered was that he was strongly attracted to her and could at least hope that she might in some small degree be attracted to him.

"What ails you now, man? Some gay girl . . ."

"—my father, Mr. Sutton."

Sutton almost dropped the book in his hands, so startled was he by the sound of Judith's voice intruding on his thoughts. He placed the book back on the shelf and turned to find her standing in the doorway of the room beside a tall lean man who was wearing the clothes of a ranch hand. What had she said?

"I'm Abe Fletcher," the man standing beside Judith announced. He strode across the room, his hand held out.

Sutton gave his name and shook hands with Fletcher.

"My daughter tells me," Fletcher said, "that you and she had already met, Mr. Sutton."

Judith said, "Mr. Sutton was trying to catch Wildfire the day we met, Father. I prevented him from doing so."

"You did what?" Fletcher cried, turning to face his daughter.

Smiling, Judith linked her arm in her father's. "I'm afraid Mr. Sutton might still be angry with me for what I did the day we met."

"No, Miss Fletcher, I'm not," Sutton assured her while wondering if he was telling her the truth. He wasn't sure.

"I am glad to hear that, Mr. Sutton," Judith said. "I thought I had made an enemy of you for sure that day."

Sutton couldn't conceive of himself as being the enemy of anyone as attractive as Judith Fletcher and he was trying to find a way—one that would not sound foolish, or worse, impudent—of saying so when her father boomed, "Why in the world didn't you let Mr. Sutton catch that damned—excuse me, my dear—that darned horse so we could all be done with him and the havoc he has been wreaking all across this land of ours?"

"I told you when we first met, Mr. Sutton," Judith said, "that my father has no love for mustangs, Wildfire most particularly." She gave her father a mockingly stern look.

He absently patted her hand and spluttered, "Why in the world should I have any love for that beast and his destructive habits? He and his herd—and all the feral horses in this area—will ruin the range before long, and it will take years—years, do you hear me—to recover. Which is not to mention the ominous fact that it will never recover if those damned—excuse me, my dear—darned horses are not gotten rid of once and for all."

"I ran into another man—another cattle rancher name of Mel Dunbar," Sutton said, "who feels pretty much the same way you do, Mr. Fletcher, about the horse herds."

"Mel and I do not always see eye to eye on matters," Fletcher said, "but on this matter of the wild herds we both agree they should be annihilated."

"They very well might be," Sutton said. "I read in a newspaper in Virginia City where I've come from that the state legislators have passed a bill that'll let the army come in here and shoot as many horses—unbranded ones, I mean—as it can."

"I know about that and I'm grateful to our enlightened lawmakers for passing that bill," Fletcher said. "It will, I am convinced, prove to be a godsend. Anything that will preserve the range for legitimate business interests will be most welcome, I can assure you, Mr. Sutton."

" 'Legitimate business interests,' " Judith repeated, frowning at her father. "What about the horses? Don't they have legitimate interests too—such as the right to live?"

"They are not productive, Judith," Fletcher said solemnly. "They do only harm and not the slightest bit of good to anyone, not even themselves."

"I suppose you call Asher's Cannery and Tannery that has opened in Palisade a legitimate business interest," Judith said, her tone heated.

"Of course I do," Fletcher quickly responded. "Asher runs a business that is badly needed. He employs people so that they may provide for their families. It is only incidental that he is doing ranchers like myself some good in the process of conducting his business."

"You mentioned that this fellow, Asher, runs a cannery and tannery, Miss Fletcher," Sutton interjected. "What's that got to do with the wild horse herds?"

"Mr. Asher," Judith replied. "pays horse hunters seventy-five cents for the saddle and hindquarters of wild horses and fifty cents for their hides. He boils the meat in a hot spring near his plant, then salts and hermetically seals it in cans. He makes, I am given to understand, a great deal of money shipping his cans of horsemeat—which, incidentally, he mislabels as wild goat meat—as far away as China, Japan, and the Philippine Islands. Some he sells in Europe. Some goes to gourmet restaurants in such Eastern cities as Boston, Philadelphia, and New York.

"The hides he sells to tannery representatives from out of state—those hides he himself does not sell locally, that is. Why, only last week, Mr. Asher contracted with a buyer from Kansas for one thousand hides for which the buyer agreed to pay one dollar and eighty cents apiece. For horse manes and tails, the same buyer agreed to pay three cents a pound."

"I say good luck to Mr. Asher," Fletcher declared bluntly. "May his business thrive and prosper."

"I notice, Father, that you make no mention of the

fact that Mr. Asher's horse hunters have shot and killed some of our branded horses during their rampages."

"Rampages, my dear? Come now. It isn't as bad as all that."

"Four of our horses are dead, their hides taken by Mr. Asher's horse hunters," Judith persisted.

"I know that," her father admitted. "An unfortunate mistake on the part of some of those overzealous young men Asher has hired. But the fact remains that they are taking their toll of the feral horses and that is the most important thing. I am almost willing to believe at this stage of the game that the range will be saved after all."

Sutton said, "Mr. Fletcher, all this talk about Asher's operation, it sounds like it has to do with why I came here this morning to see you."

"I have been wondering why you came to see me, Mr. Sutton."

"It's about Wildfire, Mr. Fletcher. You see, I've been hired by a man who is a racetrack operator and horse breeder from back East to catch Wildfire for him. I've been trying hard to do that but with no luck so far. I almost had him yesterday but a man who works for you by the name of Stoner started shooting at him. I had to stop him from killing Wildfire and while I was doing that, Wildfire got away from me."

"Ah," sighed Fletcher. "I think I see now the reason for your visit, Mr. Sutton. You don't want Wildfire killed."

"No, sir, I don't. Not by Stoner or anybody else either, for that matter. I came calling on you today to ask if you'd order Stoner not to kill Wildfire. I offered to pay him twice what you would have paid him for killing Wildfire but he wouldn't take me up on my offer. Said he had a personal grudge against Wildfire that he intended to settle by killing him."

"Yes, I'm aware of that," Fletcher said. "It seems the stallion and his herd tried to kill Stoner. Or so Stoner thinks, at any rate."

"Well, like I said, Mr. Fletcher," Sutton continued, "what with the cannery and tannery Asher is running and ranchers like yourself and Dunbar out to rid the range of the mustangs and the army fixing to get mixed up in the mess too—I don't stand much of a chance of getting my hands on Wildfire before somebody somewhere goes and does him in. That's why I'd be obliged to you if you'd tell Stoner to keep away from Wildfire and just let him be."

"I would like to be able to oblige you, Mr. Sutton," Fletcher said, "but I'm afraid I cannot do so."

"Oh, Father!" Judith cried. "You would be doing me a favor too if you ordered Stoner to leave Wildfire alone. You know—I've told you many times how much I want to see that horse remain alive."

Fletcher turned to his daughter. "I know your sentiments in the matter quite well, Judith. And you know mine. Wildfire is responsible for the loss of more of my mares than I can keep track of. You know how he comes here—and to other ranches in the area as well—and lures our mares into running off with him to join his herd. Then there is the even more important matter of the way he and his herd are ruining our range. He—"

"He is but one horse, Father," Judith pointed out, speaking heatedly again. "Surely, one horse left alive—"

Fletcher held up a hand, silencing Judith. "I have no more to say on the matter, my dear. I would be most grateful to you if you would not in the future continue to worry this subject like a dog with a bone. It is a source of continuing discord between us and I for one would prefer that we not discuss it anymore."

"But Father—"

"Judith! Enough!"

To Sutton, Judith seemed to wilt under her father's stern gaze. She said no more.

But Sutton did. "Mr. Fletcher, if you'd give me just a few days I'm pretty sure I could run Wildfire down and get him away from here and out of your hair."

"Mr. Sutton, the best I can do for you under the circumstances is to continue to protect my business interests, which I mentioned earlier, while allowing you the freedom to compete against my men in the hunt for Wildfire. Quite honestly, I would be happy to see you win the competition. Despite the fact that my daughter thinks me coldhearted and implacable on the subject of the feral horses, I would be delighted to see Wildfire taken alive and removed from the area so that he can be given a new life far away from here. I am not a bloodthirsty man, Mr. Sutton. I am, however, a determined man. One who will not let his livelihood be destroyed by forces he can—and, by God, *will*—control."

"I understand how you feel, Mr. Fletcher," Sutton said with a strong sense of disappointment. "In fact, were I in your boots, I'd no doubt take the selfsame position you're taking in this matter. I just thought I ought to come here and try to boost my chances of catching Wildfire before somebody kills him.

"I thank you for attending to me. I'm just sorry we couldn't see eye to eye on the matter. Good day to you, Mr. Fletcher." Sutton was about to bid good day to Judith as well when she said, "I'll see you out."

After shaking hands with her father, Sutton followed Judith. Once outside, she surprised him by saying, "Oh, I do wish I were a man."

He smiled and said, "I hope you won't take offense at what I'm about to say, Miss Fletcher, but I for one am glad you're not a man. It would be a crying shame if the world had to do without a woman as attractive and nice to be near as yourself."

"Why, what a nice thing to say, Mr. Sutton. I thank you for the compliment." Judith met Sutton's gaze for a moment during which neither of them spoke. Then, the anger back in her voice and flashing brightly again in her eyes, she added, "But I'm sure you knew what I meant when I said that I wish I were a man. I meant that I would ride out, capture Wildfire, and then take him far away from here. I would take him to a place where there are no stud killers or horse hunters or men like my father and Mr. Dunbar—"

"Hold on a minute, Miss Fletcher."

"Please call me Judith. And if it's alright with you, I shall call you Luke."

"That suits me fine, Judith. What I was about to say was don't be too hard on your father and Mr. Dunbar. They're both doing what they figure they've got to do and I reckon there's nobody dare blame them. They've got their ranches and their stock to protect. It's a tough life that men like your father lead. They can be wiped out just about anytime by weather or if the bottom drops out of the beef market—or by wild horses. They can't do much about the weather and neither is there a whole lot they can do to keep the price of beef up year in and year out. But they sure can rid their ranges of mustangs."

"Oh, I know you're right, Luke. I know too that my father is right in the way he thinks and in what he has been doing. I refer, of course, to the hiring of a man like Stoner. I suppose I shouldn't interfere any more than I should have interfered with you that day when you were trying to capture Wildfire."

"You're hitting close to home with those last few words of yours," Sutton said somewhat sheepishly. "It rattles me to think that then I wasn't too keen on tolerating your point of view about Wildfire. But now I can stand here and preach to you about how you ought to understand your father's position."

Judith was thoughtful for a moment. Then, "Luke, do you think you will succeed in capturing Wildfire before—" She did not complete her question.

"That's hard to say," Sutton answered. "I'm going to try my best to do so but the competition your father referred to when we were talking inside—well, it's something fierce and getting fiercer every day, it seems. I didn't even know about that Asher outfit up in Palisade until you mentioned it today."

"I suppose you could use some help in your endeavor."

"It's starting to look that way. I've got to find a way, if there is one, to keep everybody else at bay while I concentrate on trapping Wildfire."

"Perhaps I could be of help to you. Perhaps I could ride with you when you go out hunting Wildfire and, should we encounter any horse hunters or stud killers like Stoner, I could distract them while you go about capturing Wildfire."

"I do appreciate your offer of help, Judith, I truly do. But I can't accept it."

"Why not?"

"It's far too risky a business. You could get yourself hurt and hurt bad maybe. But I have to admit your plan would probably work were it put into practice."

"Do you really think it would?"

"I think it very well would on account of I'm convinced that any man would find himself distracted by
you if you should ever set your mind to doing some
distracting."

Judith blushed and looked away.

"I didn't mean to step out of line by saying what I
just did," Sutton told her softly.

"You didn't," she said as softly.

"Well, I'd best be on my way."

"If you're in the area again, Luke, I would be
pleased if you came to call."

"I expect I'll be around and about here for a spell
longer. I've been bunking with Buck Hawthorn—sort
of helping him out with his horses—while I also hunt
Wildfire."

"I know Mr. Hawthorn. Father and I have visited
his place several times on business. Father has bought
some fine horses from Mr. Hawthorn."

Judith watched as Sutton freed his horse from the
hitch-rail and stepped into the saddle. She waved to
him as he rode away and he responded by touching the
brim of his hat.

He spent the rest of the morning and most of the afternoon scouring the hills in search of Wildfire and his
herd. He rode into and out of countless canyons and
gulches where he thought the horses might have taken
shelter. He crested as many hills to survey the surrounding countryside. By the time the sun was easing
down out of the sky he had seen no sign of his quarry.

He reluctantly turned his black and headed back to
Hawthorn's cabin. Another day wasted, he thought as
he rode his weary and footsore mount down the slope
of a high hill into the pool of shadows at its base. I
keep on like this, he thought, and I'll never get to catch

that stallion for Wilson. Which means this'll be the
first time I was hired to hunt for somebody—some animal in this case—and I couldn't come up with him—it.
Well, a man can't expect to have a perfect record forever.

But the gnawing sense that he might fail in this mission made him uneasy. He wondered why. It wasn't as
if the world would end should he fail in his efforts to
capture Wildfire. But somebody was depending upon
him—Wilson in this instance—and he didn't want to
let the man down. It's more than that, though, he told
himself. What's on the block here is your pride, old
son, and you damn well know it. You don't relish the
notion of going back to Virginia City with your hat in
your hand and having to tell Wilson that Wildfire outwitted you. Or worse—that you let some stud killer or
horse hunter beat you to the animal and kill it before
you could catch it.

Well, he thought, there's nothing wrong with pride.
A man needs to have some in himself. It's what keeps
him standing straight and able to look any and every
man in the eye. It's the fuel that feeds the fire inside a
man and keeps him going day after day.

He rode on, his eyes scanning the land through
which he traveled as he let his black set its own pace.
When he came to a stream that meandered between
two hummocks, he drew rein and dismounted. Getting
down on his knees beside his horse, which had
dropped its head to drink, he filled his canteen, drank
from it, and stoppered it.

He resumed his journey as the sun slid out of sight
behind a mountain range on his left. He was within a
few miles of Hawthorn's cabin when he caught his
first whiff of the strong scent, borne by the breeze that
was blowing across the land.

It was immediately familiar to him. It brought back to him grim memories of a time he had come upon a man in Mexico who had been dead for days on a barren plain. The bloated body of the man had fallen prey to buzzards, coyotes, flies, and ants. Its putrid stench was the same as the one he was smelling now.

He followed the revolting odor for several minutes, seeking its source. It grew stronger, almost making him gag. When he emerged from a grove of oak trees into a flat valley he found what he had been looking for.

He drew rein and, with his hands clasping his saddle horn, sat his saddle and stared at the scattered corpses of horses which littered the valley floor. It was easy to see that they had died from gunshots; their bodies lay in a ragged line running from east to west as they had tried to run from danger.

They were on the run alright, he thought, when they were shot. He breathed shallowly in order to keep at bay the nausea that was threatening to undo him at any moment. The hideless carcasses were heaps of bloody meat on the ground. Moving among them, their hands wet and red, were men wearing bloodstained clothes and carrying long knives. Two wagons stood on one edge of the line of slaughtered horses, both of them piled high with horse hides.

Sutton rode into the valley and stopped beside one of the wagons.

"Howdy," one of the men greeted him cordially.

"Howdy," he responded. "You fellows, it looks like, aren't taking any of the meat, just the hides. I'd heard that Asher's cannery and tannery was buying both—meat and skins."

"You heard right, mister," the man said. "But we ain't selling to Asher. We're working for a man name of Bill Hopkins up in Palisade. He's a tanner from Texas. He pays us three bucks a hide and to hell with the meat. At that rate, we make more money selling hides than we would if we sold both the meat and skins along with the tails and manes to Asher."

"Looks like you made a good kill here."

"Not bad," the man agreed, surveying the corpses. "But we did even better last week, a lot better. We skinned forty-one head then."

"Got a question for you."

"Ask it. I'll answer it for you if I can."

"Was one of the horses you boys killed a golden stallion? One that stands about fifteen hands high and is as powerful as a locomotive?"

The man, as he pondered Sutton's question, took off his hat and scratched his head while the knife in his hand dripped blood. Finally: "There was some buckskins we killed, if that's what you mean."

Sutton shook his head. "This stud's a golden color. He's not yellow or a dun. If you saw him you'd not be likely to forget him."

"I can't swear to it but I don't think we skinned any horse that looked like that. Most of what we got were the weak sisters of the two herds we chased last week and today. Most of them was mares and foals which, you maybe might know, are the first to throw down their tails and drop out of the running when a herd's being chased."

"I'm obliged to you for answering my question." Sutton rode away from the hide peelers as they continued about their bloody business, hoping fervently that the man he had just spoken to was right and that none of the horses his group had killed was Wildfire.

SEVEN

THAT NIGHT, as Sutton sat outside the cabin with Hawthorn following the satisfying supper the older mustanger had cooked, he sighed and said, "It looks, Buck, like the odds against me catching Wildfire have more than doubled since I got here."

"That's a fact," Hawthorn agreed, puffing placidly on a pipe.

"It seems like everybody in the whole wide world has heard there's a profit of one kind or another to be made out of coming to Nevada and shooting mustangs."

"Ay-yuh. They'll put us both out of business should they keep at it like they seem hell-bent on doing."

Sutton was taken aback by Hawthorn's words. He had not, until that moment, thought any farther than his own problem concerning his hunt for Wildfire. But now he realized quite clearly, as a result of what Hawthorn had just said, that the stud killers and horse hunters and hide peelers were even more of a threat to the aging mustanger who had so generously befriended him.

"If they get rid of all the mustangs," he said, "what will you do, Buck?"

"Well, maybe they won't kill every last one of them," Hawthorn answered. Then he laughed and in the sound was more than a trace of bitterness. But his expression remained calm as he continued, "There's not much I can do other than what I've been doing. I don't know much about figuring out sums or other such book learning. I never went past the second grade when I was growing up. Had me a daddy who was always on the move, which got worse—or better, depending upon your point of view—after my ma died. My, but he was a fiddle-footed man if ever there was one. I never stayed long enough in one place to go to school much. Even when I did go I was too restless to learn. Couldn't sit still. Or maybe it was that I was just plain stupid."

Sutton smiled.

Hawthorn blew a cloud of smoke into the night, momentarily masking the light of several fireflies that were flying past him at the time. "My daddy was a worker and I don't mean at the kinds of things you learn to do from books. He sharecropped here and there. He worked on a railroad. He was even a deckhand on a riverboat for a year till he got fired for getting drunk and fighting.

"The point I'm making is, I take after him. I like to work with my hands. I like being outside under the sun or in the rain—it don't much matter to me. I suppose if worst comes to worst, I could hire on at a ranch somewhere and live out what's left of my days in a bunkhouse. It wouldn't be such a bad life. But to tell you the truth, I'd miss being my own man and master. I am, you may have noticed, an independent kind of cuss."

"As a matter of fact, Buck, I have noticed that about you."

It was Hawthorn's turn to smile.

"I'm like you in more ways than one," Sutton volunteered. "I like to be on the move most of the time. I find it hard as a whore's heart to stay put for long in any one place."

"You told me you was living in Virginia City. You don't look one bit like a city boy to me, Luke, not with those horseman's boots and those jeans so worn the wind might blow them right off you with its next gust that you're wearing. So how come—"

"How come I live in the city?" Sutton leaned back against the cabin wall, crossed his ankles, folded his arms, and answered, "I just sort of landed there at the end of a long hard trail I was traveling. I'd meant to go back to where I was born and brung up down in Texas but—well, let's just say that things had changed while I was off finding out what was over the mountain and around the next bend in the crick. So I stayed in Virginia City which is, I admit, a little like a preacher trying to make himself to home in a saloon."

"What do you plan on doing about that stud, Luke?"

"There's nothing I can do but keep on looking for him and hoping no one finds him before I do." Sutton paused, recalling his brief encounter with the hide peelers. He told Hawthorn about it, concluding with, "Maybe Wildfire's already dead."

"It's possible he is. But I for one doubt it. That stallion's too clever by half to get himself shot down by a bunch of boys who just shoot into a crowd of horses hoping to hit something." Hawthorn gave Sutton a sharp look. "Do you think he's dead?"

"Nope, I don't. Somehow or other, I just can't imagine—or maybe bring myself to imagine—him being dead. A horse like him—it somehow seems like a critter that fine won't—shouldn't ever have to—die."

Both men were silent for several minutes, each of them lost in his own thoughts.

Then Sutton said, "I think I'll turn in, Buck. I plan to get an early start tomorrow."

"You want me to ride out with you tomorrow, Luke?" Hawthorn asked as Sutton got to his feet and stretched.

"I don't want to take you away from your work, Buck."

"Hell, son, mustanging *is* my work. But if you don't want me—"

Sutton, as Hawthorn's words trailed away, heard the note of plaintiveness in the older man's voice. "Buck, I can't think of anybody I need more than you. With your brains and my brawn, the pair of us are sure to catch Wildfire."

"Or die in the attempt."

"Die?"

"Those stud killers—there are tales told around these parts of their bullets going astray and winding up inside some softhearted cowboy who was just foolish enough to try to stop them from doing what they were doing—namely, killing mustangs."

"Well, be that as it may be," Sutton said, "they'll get something more than they bargained for when they come up against the two of us. I'm just bullheaded and mean enough to go up against them if there's ten to my one. And you, Buck, from what I know about you so far, why, I'd say you're a man who'd charge hell with only a bucket of water in his hands. So those stud killers had best beware when they see the pair of us coming their way."

Sutton, grinning, went inside, the sound of Hawthorn's amused laughter trailing him.

He was roused from sleep some time later by the sound of someone pounding on the cabin door.

In the bunk on the other side of the room, Hawthorn thrashed about in his blanket for a moment and then got up and started for the door. He muttered a vivid oath as he collided in the darkness with a chair. Shoving it out of his way, he yelled, "Don't tear down the goddamn door! I'm coming!"

Sutton sat up and pulled on his trousers as Hawthorn unbolted and opened the door, letting a little moonlight into the dark room.

The door slammed shut.

"Who is it?" Sutton asked as he pulled on his boots. "Who's out there?"

"That Fletcher woman," Hawthorn answered. "The woman hasn't a shred of common decency. Here she comes riding up here in the middle of the night and me in my drawers. It ain't decent, I tell you."

"I'll let her in," Sutton said as he made his cautious way through the darkness, arms outstretched to feel his way to the door.

"Don't!" Hawthorn ordered as he fumbled about in the darkness. "I can't find my pants!"

"I'll light the lamp," Sutton offered.

"Don't!" Hawthorn ordered again. "She'll see me through the window!"

"I kind of doubt that she'll want to peep at you through the window, Buck, but, alright, I won't light the lamp. I'll go outside and talk to her."

"Where the hell did I put them?" Hawthorn mumbled to himself as he continued searching for his trousers in the darkness, which was only momentarily and partially dispelled as Sutton opened the cabin door and stepped outside, closing the door behind him.

"Oh, Luke, it's you!" Judith Fletcher exclaimed. "Was that Mr. Hawthorn who just slammed the door on me? I couldn't see him clearly."

"That was Buck."

"Why wouldn't he let me in?"

"You caught him with his modesty showing. He's in his underwear. That's why he slammed the door when he saw it was you out here."

"Oh. I suppose I should have waited until morning to come here. But I couldn't. Morning might have been too late."

"What might you mean by that?" Sutton asked, suppressing a yawn and the urge to stretch the lethargy that was the legacy of sleep from his limbs. "Too late for what?"

"Earlier tonight, Mr. Dunbar rode over to our ranch. It seems Wildfire and his herd stampeded Mr. Dunbar's cattle last night and, he told Father, killed nearly two dozen head in the process. That, he said, was the third time this month that he has lost stock in such a way to Wildfire. He has, he said, lost a total of nearly fifty head that way. He was very upset."

"I've no doubt he was. No cattleman can put up with losses like that for very long—not if he intends to stay in business, he can't."

"Mr. Dunbar knew that Father had also suffered losses—though not such great ones—for the same reason."

"Wildfire and his herd."

Judith nodded. "Mr. Dunbar said he had come to the conclusion that it was time to act to stop what he called the herd's depredations."

"From what I saw the other day when I ran into Dunbar and some of his riders, he has been acting. They were all shooting at some mustangs they had trapped in a corral Buck and me built at a water hole Buck says is favored by Wildfire. They killed every one of those horses."

"Yes, I know that Mr. Dunbar and his hands have been killing feral horses. But what he said he believed was necessary now was a concerted effort on the part of all the ranchers in the vicinity to wipe out Wildfire and his herd. Individual men or even groups of men, he said, was too much of a scattergun approach. He wanted, he said, to make war on the herd, and for a war, he said, an army and a battle plan were needed."

"What did your father say to that?"

"At first, Father was reluctant to go along because he said he wasn't sure he agreed with Mr. Dunbar that such drastic action was really necessary. Mr. Dunbar insisted that no other kind but the drastic kind would work at this point.

"Father explained that he had hired Stoner to shoot Wildfire and as many other feral horses as possible. Mr. Dunbar dismissed that action as, in his words, 'ineffectual and insignificant.' He said he had already visited the other ranchers in the area and all but one of them had agreed to participate in an organized attempt to wipe out Wildfire and his herd. He said he hoped Father wasn't going to let him down. Actually, I don't think Father wanted to have anything to do with the plan but Mr. Dunbar, in my opinion, more or less shamed him into participating in it.

"I came here after Mr. Dunbar had left and Father had gone to bed to tell you about their plan, so that you would have a chance to catch Wildfire before they can kill him."

"How do they plan to go about the hunt, do you know?" Sutton asked as a chill went through him that was not caused by the cool night air.

"They plan to ride through Wildfire's home range, which is in the mountainous central part of the county, as I believe you know. You and I first met at the southern end of that range, if you recall. They intend to spread out and ride north through Pine Valley. They will, along the way, search through the canyons and other likely places the herd might take refuge, which are scattered throughout the mountains. They will travel past Pole Creek and up to and even beyond the town of Palisade in the north if necessary."

"Sounds like they really mean to beat the bushes for sure."

"Mr. Dunbar is determined to wipe out the herd once and for all," Judith said sadly. "Some of the men, Mr. Dunbar told Father, himself included, are taking Sharps' rifles with them. I understand such guns can do a great deal of damage."

"That's a fact. That .50 caliber gun is a favorite weapon of buffalo hunters. I've seen it knock big bull buffaloes off their feet at a range of up to six hundred yards."

"Mr. Dunbar said it's an accurate weapon too, by and large," Judith said, her voice still doleful. "He claims that's because of the gun's telescopic sight. Oh, Luke, Wildfire doesn't stand a chance, does he?"

"I don't think you really believe that, Judith. If you did, you wouldn't have come here to me with the news of the hunt."

"I must confess that I came here with more hope than any real belief that you or anyone else for that matter could stop what I have begun to believe in the last few hours is the inevitable. Maybe I just shouldn't care. Maybe it doesn't matter whether Wildfire lives or dies. But somehow I just can't bring myself to believe that. I don't *want* to believe it."

"What time are your father and Dunbar and the others setting out after the herd?"

"They plan to meet at Mr. Dunbar's ranch and leave from there about ten o'clock in the morning."

"I appreciate you coming here to tell me about this, Judith. I'd planned to get an early start tomorrow morning and go hunting Wildfire with Buck. Now that I know what's afoot, thanks to you, I'll just leave earlier than I had planned to. That way I ought to be able to increase my odds of getting to Wildfire before your father and the others do."

"I wish you luck, Luke—the very best of luck."

"I'll need my share of it this time out, that's for sure."

Sutton stood facing Judith, neither of them moving, both of them looking into each other's eyes. He wanted to do something to erase the lines of worry he saw on her face. He wanted to say something that would ease her mind. He wanted to . . .

He hesitated only briefly before taking Judith in his arms and holding her close to him as he kissed her on the lips. She did not respond at first but then, as his grip on her tightened and his lips remained on hers, her arms went around him and their kiss deepened.

Moments later, as Sutton started to release her, Judith's hand rose. She cupped the back of his head, preventing him from ending their kiss.

Behind Sutton, Hawthorn opened the cabin door. He immediately stepped back and slammed the door when he saw what was happening outside.

Sutton and Judith, startled by the loud sound of the slamming door, separated.

"Buck?" Sutton called out.

The door eased open and Hawthorn's head appeared around the jamb. "I found my pants," he said. "I can come out now if you folks don't think three's a crowd."

"Judith," Sutton said, "came to tell me that her father and Mel Dunbar and a whole bunch of other fellows are fed up with Wildfire and the way him and his herd's been stampeding and killing their cattle. They're going to try to wipe them out once and for all."

Hawthorn whistled through his teeth. "That puts you on the hot spot, don't it, Luke? I mean if they kill Wildfire—"

"I've got to see to it that they don't, Buck," Sutton said quickly. "I'm going to get the rest of my clothes and ride out after that stallion."

"Now?" an incredulous Hawthorn asked.

"My father and the other men will be out hunting the herd by mid-morning," Judith informed Hawthorn.

"Well, then," he said, "looks like time's a-wasting, Luke. Let's go wake up our horses and be on our way."

"Go get them, will you, Buck? I'll be right with you."

When Hawthorn had gone for the horses, Sutton again embraced Judith and kissed her. "I thank you again for coming here and telling me what Dunbar has planned. You might have saved Wildfire's life."

"I do fervently hope so," Judith whispered. "Promise me you'll be careful, Luke. As much as I want to see Wildfire saved, I don't want you to be hurt trying to save him."

"I'll watch my step," Sutton promised; then, after Judith had boarded her horse and departed, he joined Hawthorn.

The mustanger had both horses saddled and bridled. He left them with Sutton while he went back into the cabin to get some provisions to take with them.

Sutton was waiting in front of the cabin when Hawthorn came out with two gunnysacks, one of which he handed to Sutton.

"Packed some corn bread and some potatoes we can roast," he announced as he and Sutton stored the sacks in their saddle bags.

Minutes later they were riding out, heading for Wildfire's home range.

They spent the hours that remained of the night searching in vain for some sign of the horse herd. They reached the water hole they had earlier encircled with canvas when the first faint signs of rosy daylight streaked the sky just above the horizon.

"Told you there weren't no use in coming here," Hawthorn muttered as both men drew rein and stared inside the corral at the rotting corpses of the horses which had been shot by Dunbar and his riders. "No mustang'll come within a mile of this water hole now, not with those dead animals in there."

"I just wanted to check the place on the off chance that they might have come here anyway," Sutton said.

"My oh my, don't those mustangs *stink* though? Let's get out of here."

"Where's the water hole nearest to here?" Sutton asked as both men moved out.

"Pole Creek's about two miles east of here. You figure we'll find them there?"

"Well, they generally drink in the mornings and they've got to go someplace to do it. Since the water hole we corraled is not to their liking anymore, I reckon our chances of finding the herd where there's water are at least good."

The sun, bisected by the flat line of the horizon, was rising as they reached Pole Creek and found only deer drinking from the clear water. At their approach the

deer fled, their white tails bobbing, leaving only silence behind them.

"Let's ride the crick," Sutton suggested.

"Might as well."

They rode north on the left side of Pole Creek, both
men squinting into the bright distance as the sun
cleared the horizon and began to warm them and the
land around them. They saw no sign of the herd.

But an hour later, still riding the creek, they spotted
several horses on the far side of the water.

"They're coming this way," Hawthorn observed.
"We'd best take cover somewheres."

He moved out, heading for a hummock not far
away. When he glanced over his shoulder and saw that
Sutton wasn't following him, he called out, "Those
horses, should they spot you, won't come any closer no
matter how thirsty they might happen to be."

Sutton stood up in his stirrups, pulled his hat down
low on his forehead to block out the sun's rays, and
peered at the approaching mustangs.

A moment later, he resumed his seat in the saddle
and beckoned to Hawthorn. "Wildfire's not with that
bunch," he said when Hawthorn had rejoined him.

"You sure do got good eyes," Hawthorn marveled.
"I couldn't spot him from here if he was wearing spats
and a derby hat."

They moved on then and continued riding the
creek. Sutton was keenly and uncomfortably aware of
the passing of time as the sun rose higher in the sky.
He began to sweat. By mid-morning, his shirt was
sticking to his back and he had taken to removing his
hat from time to time to run a thumb around its inner
band, wiping it free of sweat.

"There!" Hawthorn suddenly yelled and pointed.

Sutton saw them. He estimated that there were at

least fifty horses in the herd. He recognized the white
mare leading them as the same one that had been leading Wildfire's herd the last time he had encountered
them. He strained his eyes, trying to see if Wildfire
was with the herd.

At first he couldn't see the stallion in the mass of
bodies galloping toward the creek. But then he spotted
the golden stallion at the rear of the herd. Wildfire's
mane was flying and his head was bobbing up and
down as he followed his mares and foals down a slope
toward the water.

"Let's circle around behind them," Hawthorn suggested.

Sutton shook his head. "I'll go get him my own
self," he told Hawthorn.

Hawthorn's eyes widened in surprise. "I come way
the hell out here to help you and now you turn around
and tell me you've got no need of me?"

"You got me wrong, Buck. I didn't mean I had no
need of you. I do. What I want you to do for me, if
you're willing, is this. Go back—"

"*Go back?*"

"Find Dunbar and the others if you can. When and
if you do, tell them some cock-and-bull story about
how you've been trailing Wildfire. Get them to follow
you. Lead them as far away from here as you can."

"That's not a bad way to buy yourself some time
which you might very well need with what you've got
facing you, Luke. I'll do it."

"I'll meet you back at the cabin. I don't know when
exactly but I'll be there sooner or later."

The two men parted then, with Hawthorn heading
back the way they had come and Sutton riding in the
opposite direction to disappear in a grove of birches.

He rode through the trees for more than a half-mile.

When he emerged from them, he forded Pole Creek and rode at a right angle to it, intending to follow Hawthorn's strategy, which the mustanger had suggested earlier, of circling around and coming in behind the herd.

He made his turn and was riding a trail that ran parallel to Pole Creek but was almost a mile from it, when he heard the sound of horses. For a moment he thought Wildfire and his herd had left the creek and were retracing their steps. But, as he topped a rise, he saw that the sounds he had heard were being made by a long line of mounted troopers who were moving in the direction of Pole Creek.

He rode down the rise, intending to overtake the troopers. He knew why they were there. There was no escaping the knowledge. He had been warned by Violet Wilson; she had shown him the article that had been published in *The Territorial Enterprise,* which told of the Nevada legislature's decision to use the army to help exterminate the wild horse herds.

He caught up with the officer leading the line who was flanked by a sergeant. Noting the man's insignia, he searched his memory for the name that had been mentioned in the *Enterprise* article. Carruthers? No. Carstairs? No. Then it came to him—Carrington.

"Captain Carrington," he said as he rode beside the man toward Pole Creek, "I take it you're out here after mustangs."

"Yes, we are. How is it, sir, that you know my name?"

"I read about you in a newspaper in Virginia City. The article I read said you'd been assigned by the army to come out here to shoot yourself some horses."

"That is correct."

"My name, Captain, is Luke Sutton. I came out here

from Virginia City to run mustangs. Well, that's not exactly right. What I mean is I came out here to run one mustang in particular but so far I've had to run both him and his herd—so I suppose I was right the first time."

"What is your point, Mr. Sutton?"

"My point. Yes, sir, I was just getting to it. Are you after the herd that left those tracks you seem to be following?"

"We are. Of what interest is that to you, Mr. Sutton?"

"Well, Captain, the herd-master of that bunch is a stud folks around here call Wildfire. Now, he happens to be the horse I came here to catch. If you and your men start shooting at him, you might kill him and then where will I be? So what I'd like to do is make you a proposition."

"A proposition, Mr. Sutton?"

"You and your men back off for a bit. Just long enough for me to start running Wildfire and get him away from his herd. Then you fellows can move in and start shooting to your heart's content. How's that sound to you?"

Captain Carrington exchanged glances with his sergeant. Neither man spoke for a moment. Then Carrington said, "I've seen the stallion you mentioned and I've been told about him by ranchers and others. He is a quite remarkable example of horseflesh."

"He is that, Captain," Sutton agreed enthusiastically.

"It would be a shame to kill him."

"It would be indeed, Captain."

"I've not, to tell you the plain truth, Mr. Sutton, got the heart for this assignment. I have spent my entire army career in the cavalry. I joined the cavalry initially in part because I have, ever since I was a boy on our farm in Nebraska, loved horses. It is extremely difficult therefore for me to order the slaughter of these animals."

"I can understand your position, Captain. I have a fondness for good horseflesh myself."

"But orders are orders, Mr. Sutton, and I am a soldier so I must obey the orders I am given. I have obeyed them. My troopers have killed over a hundred horses in Elko and White Pine counties to date. We will kill more. Specifically, in this instance, I am referring to the horse known as Wildfire as well as his herd."

"Captain, I know all about orders and the army and so on. I was a soldier during the war myself. But what I'm asking you to do—*all* I'm asking—is for you to just hold off on the killing just long enough to give me a chance to split Wildfire from his herd and run him away from here. Then you and your men can move in and commence the killing."

"Mr. Sutton, my men and I are camped a mile south of the town of Palisade. Do you know where Palisade is located?"

"I do. It's north of here."

"This is the farthest south we have ranged since arriving in the area. That is because the herd we have been pursuing has twice this morning eluded us. If we don't complete our job soon, we will not be able to return to our camp by nightfall, and I don't wish to inflict that unnecessary hardship on my men. But more importantly, and more germane to the matter at hand, is the fact that, were I to grant your request, it could very well result in your frightening the herd and causing them to stampede.

"Now I most certainly would not want that to hap-

pen because then my men would be forced to race after the herd, tiring them and their mounts even more
than they already are and perhaps losing the herd in
the process."

"I take it you're saying you won't give me the
chance I'm asking you for."

"I'm afraid I cannot, Mr. Sutton."

"Then, Captain, what I'm going to have to do is take
it."

Sutton gripped his horse hard with both legs and
moved it out into a fast gallop, heading for Pole Creek
and Wildfire. But he had not gone more than a hundred yards when he found himself flanked by two of
Carrington's troopers who had caught up with him.
Both men had their revolvers in their hands. When
they ordered him to halt, he had no choice. He halted.

Carrington and the other troopers rode up to where
Sutton was sitting his saddle, his hands in the air.

"Now that you have taken Mr. Sutton into custody
as I ordered," Carrington said, addressing the two
troopers who had apprehended Sutton, "please keep
him under guard until we have completed the destruction of the horse herd we have been trailing."

EIGHT

"CAPTAIN," Sutton said and, when Carrington had turned in his direction, continued, "I reckon I was a little bit hasty just now in saying what I did about taking matters into my own hands."

"I would most certainly agree with that, Mr. Sutton," Carrington responded icily.

"There's still time—and a way—to work things out between the two of us," Sutton persisted. "You said yourself, Captain, that you didn't have the heart for shooting horses—"

"But let me remind you, Mr. Sutton, that I also said I had my orders and that I intended to obey them to the letter and to the very best of my ability."

Your orders be damned, Sutton thought, but he said, "You wouldn't be disobeying those orders of yours that you set such store by, Captain. Not if you gave me my head and let me cut Wildfire out of the herd before you commence your shooting."

"Mr. Sutton," Carrington said somewhat wearily, "we have gone over this ground once. I see no point in doing so again."

"But Captain—"

Sutton's words were rendered inaudible by Carrington's smartly barked orders, which instructed the two troopers flanking Sutton to disarm and stand guard over him, and directed the remaining troopers to move out in pursuit of their prey.

As Carrington and his men rode out, the trooper on Sutton's right removed Sutton's revolver from its holster and his Winchester from the saddle boot.

Sutton, as he continued sitting his saddle and watching the troopers ride toward Pole Creek, asked, "Is it alright with you two boys if I put my hands down now?"

The troopers exchanged glances. Then the one who had taken Sutton's guns nodded.

Sutton lowered his hands, his eyes still fixed on the backs of the departing troopers in the distance.

"You almost had him, Sutton," the trooper on Sutton's left remarked. "If you had just kept at the captain, I think he might have given in and let you have your way with the horse—that Wildfire. Carrington's got no stomach for this job. Last time we started shooting at a bunch of wild horses, he lost his dinner, not to mention some of his pride. He went red as the stripes in the flag when he done it in front of all of us."

"Can't say as I blame him much," said the other trooper. "It's a dirty business, no two ways around that. Shooting those horses and then leaving them lying all over the place to stink and draw carrion-eaters —it's a bad business."

"Seeing as that's how you feel," Sutton said to the trooper who had just spoken, "maybe you and your friend could see your way clear to give me back my guns, let me go, and—"

Sutton's suggestion was met by scornful laughter from the trooper on Sutton's left. "If we did that, Captain Carrington would shoot *us* instead of those horses."

Well, thought Sutton, it was worth a try even if it didn't pan out like I hoped it would. He turned his head slightly, noting that his revolver was now resting in the waistband of the trooper who had taken it from him, his rifle in the crook of the same man's left arm. He shifted his gaze again to the other trooper and saw that the man was watching the last of the troopers disappear down the far side of a rise.

Slowly, in order not to attract the attention of the trooper on his left, he eased his left foot out of its stirrup. Then, ostentatiously folding both hands around his saddle horn, he said, "It looks like they're coming back."

"Coming back?" echoed the man who was still staring off into the distance. "I don't see nobody coming back."

"You see them, don't you?" Sutton asked the man on his right, who had his guns.

The trooper turned his head and squinted into the distance. "I don't see—"

He never got to finish what he had been about to say because Sutton chose that moment to seize the coiled rope that hung from his saddle horn. He used it to strike the trooper a blow on the side of the head that knocked him out of his saddle.

Before he hit the ground, Sutton thrust out his left foot and kicked the other trooper's mount, causing it to dash forward and almost lose its startled rider.

Sutton leaped from the saddle, seized his guns from the fallen trooper he had struck with his rope, and ordered the other trooper to halt.

But the trooper whose horse had bolted turned and, as he fought for the control of his prancing mount, tried to take aim at Sutton. Before the man could take proper aim, however, Sutton shot his hat from his head. "Drop it!" he yelled, and the trooper promptly threw his gun to the ground. He raised his hands and as he did so his horse bolted again.

Sutton bent down and picked up the revolver that the trooper had dropped when he fell from his horse. Then, as the still-stunned trooper propped himself up on his elbows and tried to focus his eyes, Sutton disarmed him and slapped the hindquarters of the man's mount to send it galloping away into the distance.

He booted his Winchester and stored the troopers' guns in his saddlebag. Then he stepped into the saddle and went galloping off in the direction of Pole Creek, holstering his revolver as he rode.

When he caught sight of Carrington and his men up ahead, he swerved to the left so that Carrington, riding at the head of the column of men, would not immediately see him when he caught up with the line. As he drew closer to the men, they vanished in the roiling dust their column was raising.

Sutton welcomed the dust. It kept the troopers from seeing him and, because the dust itself revealed their whereabouts, he was able to keep track of the progress they were making.

He heard the sound of shots up ahead of him and a moment later saw flashes of fire amid the shifting dust; this meant, he knew, that the troopers had sighted and were firing at the herd. He rode on, a sense of desperation riding with him. He came abreast of the column and then, a moment later, rode past it as he continued heading toward Pole Creek where, he was now able to see, the shuddering bodies of several dying mares and a filly lay at the edge of the water.

He heard a shout behind him. He hunkered down in the saddle, bending forward in order to keep his head close to his black's neck. He blinked the sweat that flew from the animal's body out of his eyes and rode on as the surviving horses raced in every direction along the bank of the creek. Most of them followed the white mare that habitually led the herd but others scattered, some running toward the troopers in their fright, only to be downed and left to die where they fell.

Where is he? Sutton asked himself over and over again, the words a pounding rhythm in his mind. Had Wildfire escaped? Or had he left the herd before the troopers arrived? He could see no sign of the stallion. An awful thought occurred to him. Had Wildfire been shot? Killed? He took another hurried look at the dead and dying horses on the ground, some of which were lying half submerged in the creek. Wildfire was not among them. Then—where?

He finally caught sight of the horse in the midst of the others which were following the white mare as she frantically tried to lead them to safety. He turned his horse and headed after them as they raced up a slope to the south.

He almost held his breath as he continued trailing the horses—specifically Wildfire, who by now had eased himself out of the mass of bodies and was bringing up the rear. Will those troopers back there shoot at me? he wondered. Now that I've put myself between them and the horses they're after, they just might nick me—or worse—either out of carelessness, bad shooting, or on an order from Captain Carrington.

He heard shots but they seemed distant. Glancing back over his shoulder, he saw that the troopers had formed a skirmish line and were killing the horses that remained within range of their guns. Once they've wiped out all of them, he thought, they'll be coming this way. When they come, me and Wildfire had best be long gone.

The thought lent an even greater sense of urgency to his efforts and, as a result, he began narrowing the distance between himself and his quarry. The stallion suddenly began to slow and as it did an elated Sutton speculated that it might be tiring. But such was not the case, he realized as Wildfire abruptly swung his head around to stare in Sutton's direction. The horse immediately increased its speed and bit the haunch of a mare running directly in front of it.

As Sutton drew closer to him, Wildfire, held back by the slower pace of the herd which did not—perhaps could not—match his own, changed his tactics. No longer biting the mares in front of him, he fell back at the same time that two colts dropped their tails and fell out.

He turned and raced around to the left of the herd. Flanking it now, he continued galloping, his tail popping: a sure sign that he was far from worn out—that he had, in fact, a great deal of reserve energy left for the chase.

Sutton reached the herd. He rode around it until he too was flanking the fleeing horses. Now the distance between himself and Wildfire was only a matter of yards. He began to hope, as he reached for his rope, that the time was rapidly approaching when he would land his loop on the stallion's neck and the first battle of the war between them would have been won.

But, as hope burgeoned within him, Wildfire whistled. In response to the stallion's whistle, the white mare leading the herd suddenly changed direction. Veering sharply to the left, she succeeded in turning the herd. Wildfire turned with them.

Sutton knew what was coming. He knew too that he was powerless to prevent it from happening. He nevertheless pulled hard on the reins and exerted pressure with his knees—all to no avail. The black could not turn aside in time. Sutton braced himself, swung his left leg over his saddle horn, and, pushing against the neck of his horse, threw himself from the saddle. As he hit the ground, his horse collided head-on with the mass of running horses that was the herd. The black was thrown backward and to one side. It fell to the ground, legs thrashing in the air, moments after Sutton had hit the ground.

Pain screamed through Sutton's body. But it did not stop him from rolling over several times in an effort to stay clear of the scores of hooves that were streaking past him. He coughed as dust filled his nose and entered his open mouth through which he was desperately gasping for breath.

His right shoulder and his ribs on that side were alive with pain that made him feel as if a fiery poker were raking him. His vision was blurred. The herd seemed to him to be a solid moving wall. He could not distinguish the bodies of individual horses as they ran past him, their manes and tails flying. He tried to rise, fell back. The pain flared, a blinding red flower blossoming in front of his eyes. Steadying himself while he sat swaying from side to side on the ground, he tried again to rise as the last of the herd raced past him. This time he got halfway to his feet before his legs gave out on him and he went down again. Cursing, he gritted his teeth and pushed himself up onto his knees. Putting out both arms to help balance himself, he got one foot under him, then the other. Slowly, he rose. He stood there, still swaying, his body still burning in a pit of pain, and he focused not on the pain but on the remarkable fact that he had done it: he was standing up, however unsteadily.

As his vision cleared, he saw that his black was also on its feet and standing forlornly not far away, its head drooping as it blew. He looked at the animal's legs and was relieved to see that the horse was putting weight on all four of them. None then were broken. He breathed a ragged sigh of relief.

And looked off into the distance.

The herd was rapidly disappearing around a bend nearly a mile away.

Grinding his teeth together in frustration, he took several unsteady steps toward his horse. He tried to make his mind a blank so that it would not register the pain he was feeling. His attempt failed. The pain notwithstanding, he made steady if slow progress toward his black. When he finally reached it, he leaned his forehead against its neck, which was wet with sweat, and closed his eyes, taking deep breaths.

"Coo-eee," he whispered to the black. "Coo-eee, old fellow."

Putting a foot in a stirrup, he started to step into the saddle. As he did so, his cinch slipped and the saddle slid down along the black's barrel.

Wearily, he shoved it back into place. Then he bent down, the muscles in his upper body protesting the move, and tightened the cinch. This time when he tried he made it into the saddle.

"We've got ourselves a way to go yet," he told the black. "Let's not neither one of us give up the ghost just yet, old fellow." The words were, he knew, a kind of prayer. One he had said for the black—and for himself.

The thought that his mount might give out on him before he could accomplish his purpose chilled him despite the heat of the day. It could happen, he knew. He had seen it happen to other men, although no horse he had ever ridden during his days as a mustanger had ever given out on him. But one had had the misfortune, he remembered, to step into a badger hole, which had resulted in a broken leg; this, in turn, had forced him to shoot the animal.

A lone mustanger, he knew, constantly faced the threat of losing his horse. No, not losing it. That's a beat-around-the-bush way of putting the matter. A mustanger, he thought, constantly faced the possibility of killing his mount, of having it drop dead under him during the intense stress of the chase.

That was why many mustangers worked in teams. One would run the herd for a certain distance, at which point he would drop out of the chase and another man with a fresh horse would take his place. Such a relay system, involving two, three, or even more riders, was an almost always successful way to capture wild horses. The wild ones nearly always gave out before any one of the horses used in the relay system was winded.

He rode on, letting his black trot, resisting the impulse to move any faster. Got to save him, he thought. Got to save this old horse for later when I catch up with the herd and the chase starts in all over again. And, by God, I will catch up with them. They'll slow down and stop pretty soon. Once they think they've gotten rid of me, they will. They'll need to catch their breath, same as a fox with the hounds on its tail does.

By the time he had reached the bend around which Wildfire and his herd had disappeared, he couldn't help himself. He set the black to galloping. As he rounded the bend, his view was blocked by a dense growth of trees. He noted the many broken limbs, hanging down low or lying on the ground.

Those horses bulled their way right through that forest, he told himself. He moved his black in among the trees, traveling fast now, dodging branches and weaving his way among the trees while maintaining his pace.

Minutes later he emerged from the forest, and the sibilant sighing of the trees as the wind moved among them was replaced by the sound of horses nickering softly and blowing.

There they were! Spread out and grazing on an open stretch of ground, home to a stream which wound its way through the calf-high grass and past clusters of orange-red paintbrush and blue flax.

He fought the urge to go galloping full-tilt toward the herd, cut Wildfire out of it, and drop his loop on the stallion. He fought it because he wanted to give his horse a chance to rest before the chase began again. He would wait and, while waiting, let the animal regain its breath and its strength for the ordeal that lay ahead of it.

He dismounted and hunkered down in the shadow shed by the horse, his eyes on the herd in the distance. They grazed peacefully, some of them raising their heads from time to time to stare, fascinatedly, into the distance at nothing. Their scouting movements were a sign of their alertness, and Sutton knew they were ready to stampede at the slightest sign or suspicion of threat. Wildfire prowled among his mares and their offspring like a staunch sentinel, only occasionally dropping his head to graze and then only for the briefest of moments. From his vantage point, Sutton could see that the gunshot wound that Stoner had earlier inflicted on the stallion's neck had healed.

Time passed all too slowly for Sutton as the sun even more slowly altered its position in the sky. He removed his hat and wiped the sweat from his face with the back of his hand. Then he rose and climbed back into the saddle. Patting his horse on the neck, he whispered, "You're a good fellow, a good strong fellow. Don't let me down now. I want that stud. I want him so bad my brain's about to boil just thinking about how bad I want him."

He rode out fast, heading directly for the herd. He had gone no more than a few feet when the horses became aware of his presence. They stopped grazing immediately and moved restlessly about for only moments before beginning to stampede, as Sutton had known they would. He increased his speed as Wildfire moved rapidly among his mares, herding them away. But several mares began to run in the opposite direction from that taken by the main body of the herd.

Wildfire, apparently unwilling to relinquish even a single member of his harem, set out in pursuit of them.

Sutton exulted; now he had far fewer horses to contend with and a much greater chance of catching the one horse he was after without interference from the bulk of the herd.

He changed direction and went after Wildfire, who was biting his wayward mares in an effort to turn them in the direction taken by the rest of the herd. Two of them did turn obediently but one continued on her rapid journey away from the herd.

Sutton galloped on. Within minutes he was between Wildfire and the remaining mare the stallion was trying to turn. Seeing himself suddenly cut off from the object of his pursuit, Wildfire abruptly balked, his front feet sliding along the ground as he struggled to slow his pace. Sutton rode past him and then sharply turned his black. His lariat was in his hand and he was swinging a wide loop as he rode back toward his prey.

Wildfire, abandoning the mare he had been chasing and turning swiftly, began to gallop toward the herd that was still fleeing, leaving trampled grass and crushed flowers in its ruinous wake.

Sutton went after him, his loop whining through the air above his head.

Wildfire's body was awash with white foam now as sweat poured from him. Still he kept on, his muscles rippling, his strong legs pounding the ground as he tried to make his escape from this man who, it seemed, would not let him alone, would not stop pursuing him.

Sutton carefully judged the distance between himself and the stallion. Waiting only a few more seconds, he let his loop fly through the air. When he made a perfect head catch on his first try, he couldn't help himself. Even as his rope went taut and almost jerked him out of the saddle, he let out a wordless shout of triumph. But he knew the battle was not yet over and he knew as well that the war was far from being won.

Moving closer to Wildfire to get some slack in his rope, he rode up on the stallion's left side. With a deft snap of his wrist, he flipped his rope along the right side of Wildfire's body and around the animal's flank and hindquarters just beneath its tail. Turning his black at a forty-five degree angle, he rode away from the stallion's path.

The result of his change of direction was that the roped stallion's head was twisted back so that it was facing the rear. The taut rope flipped the horse over, reversing its direction in a violent corkscrew somersault. The sound of Wildfire hitting the ground—a deep drumlike sound—was sweet in Sutton's ears.

He quickly took several dallies around his saddle horn. As he dismounted, he secured his rope with a quick half hitch. His black kept the rope taut as Wildfire, dazed, fought his way to his feet. The stallion stood there, obviously groggy from the fall it had taken, its great eyes rolling, its nostrils quivering, and the sweaty lather that coated its body falling in large white patches to the ground.

Sutton, wasting no time because he was not sure how long his horse might be able to hold Wildfire captive—the stallion, he estimated, weighed a good hundred pounds more than the black—opened his saddlebag and removed the short length of rope he had brought with him from Hawthorn's place when the two men had set out after Wildfire.

Then, as Wildfire strained at the rope that tied him to Sutton's saddle horn, the black giving no more than an inch or two of ground in the silent struggle, Sutton gingerly circled the captive stallion. When he was behind the horse, he bent down and quickly tied the length of rope tightly around the hamstring on Wildfire's right hind leg.

Darting backward then, he just barely escaped the kick the high-stepping stallion aimed at him. Smiling broadly and putting distance between himself and the stallion, he made his way back to his black. He moved his mount closer to Wildfire, thereby giving the rope some slack. Before Wildfire could take advantage of the slack, he untied the half hitch he had made and freed the rope he had dallied around his saddle horn. He let it fall to the ground.

Wildfire, the rope trailing from his neck, immediately made a dash for freedom. But he didn't go far because the rope that Sutton had tied tightly around his right hind leg crippled him and thus prevented him from running.

He stood still for a moment, not a muscle in his huge body moving. Then he swung his head around and kicked out with his bound hind leg. He snorted and twisted his body, trying to bite the leg that had so suddenly and inexplicably failed him. But his efforts were in vain. He could not reach the leg nor the rope that hobbled it.

He gave up the effort and tried again to run. This time he managed to travel nearly fifty feet. But despite the valiant effort to return to the wild, he was finally forced to halt in order to end the pain his attempted flight to freedom was causing him.

He threw back his head and screamed. To Sutton, the piercing sound seemed to blend anguish and defeat, rage and humiliation. He waited, trying not to face the feeling of pity mixed with regret that was stirring within him as he watched the proud stallion being forced to face the fact that his freedom was dead and his pride lost. But the feeling persisted, so Sutton, in an attempt to bury it beneath action, strode toward Wildfire.

When the horse saw him coming, it shied but did not run. Not at first. But then, as Sutton came closer to it, instinct took over and the stallion started to flee only to have his bound leg give out on him. He crashed to the ground and rolled over. By the time he had gotten back on his feet, Sutton was holding and tugging on the rope that was still looped around the animal's neck.

Wildfire drew back at first, but when Sutton continued pulling hard on the rope, the stallion moved toward him. Sutton, in order to cause him as little pain as possible, slowly led him back to where he had left his black. He swung into the saddle, took two dallies around his saddle horn with the rope, and then rode out with Wildfire following behind with evident and somewhat unruly reluctance.

Hawthorn's cabin first appeared to Sutton as a yellow
light blazing in the midst of utter blackness. No walls
were visible. Only the one lighted window, blazing
like a welcoming beacon under a sky full of clouds that
totally obscured the moon and stars.

Still leading Wildfire, who by now was limping
meekly in his wake, Sutton rode up to the empty corral where he drew rein. After positioning his black so
that the rope encircling Wildfire's neck was taut, he
dismounted. Removing his bowie knife from his boot,
he circled around behind the stallion. Timing his
move carefully with the movements of the stallion, he
bent down and cut through the rope that bound its
hind leg.

Wildfire responded by throwing both of his hind
legs up into the air, barely missing Sutton who went
back to the corral, opened its gate, and then climbed
back into the saddle. As Wildfire, much of his former
wildness returning, fought the rope that held him pris-
oner, Sutton rode inside the corral, forcing the captured stallion to follow him.

Once inside the enclosure, he flipped the rope several times to loosen it. Then he flipped it free of the
horse's neck. He turned his black and rode out of the
corral, slamming the gate behind him and locking it
only a moment before Wildfire, who had been coming
quickly up behind him, collided with the stout poles
and crosspieces of which the gate was built.

The stallion turned and trotted back into the center
of the corral where it stood staring in Sutton's direction, looking like the pale ghost of a horse in the darkness.

Only then, as Sutton made his way to the cabin, did
he let himself acknowledge the pain that was still ram-
pant in his right shoulder and ribs. Duller now, it was

nevertheless still there, a reminder of his battle with the stallion, a battle he had at last won.

He looked back over his shoulder. Wildfire was still standing motionless in the dark night, a faintly blond blur on black shadows. Sutton wondered why he felt no sense of triumph. He had fought hard and he had the bruises and the pain to prove it. But where was the sense of triumph he had once felt? In its place now was a feeling of vague sadness tinged with guilt.

Sadness? Guilt?

He shook his head in chagrin. I should be doing my victory dance, he thought, not lamenting the fact that I just locked up a feral fuzztail in that corral back there. I should be—

His reverie was interrupted by the opening of the cabin door. Hawthorn, lantern in hand, appeared in the doorway. Holding the lantern high and squinting into the darkness beyond its light, he called out, "Who's there?"

"It's me, Buck."

"Luke?"

Sutton moved on into the small pool of light shed by the lantern.

"Did you get him, Luke?"

"I got him."

"Where is he? Where'd you leave him?"

"In the corral."

"I emptied it out for you. I had a feeling this time you'd get him. I'll be right back. I want to get a look at him."

When Hawthorn had gone, Sutton slumped down on the wooden bench next to the door and leaned back against the cabin wall. He closed his eyes and let his arms hang down by his sides. A deep weariness overcame him.

"—he's a beaut, Luke, a real beaut and you got him, by golly!"

Sutton awoke with a start, surprised to find that he had fallen asleep. He stood up as Hawthorn grabbed his hand and pumped it.

"Congratulations, Luke! Congratulations on a job well done."

"Did you find Dunbar and Fletcher and those boys?"

A grin spread across Hawthorn's face. "Sure, I did. I led them on the longest wild-goose chase in the whole history of the world, I did!"

"I'm obliged to you, Buck. If you hadn't've kept those boys out of my hair I might not have been able to catch Wildfire and bring him back here."

"When are you fixing to start in on breaking him?"

"In the morning. But right now, Buck, all I want to do is find my bed and flop down on it. I'm bushed."

NINE

THE FOLLOWING MORNING Sutton stood with Hawthorn outside the corral as both men watched Wildfire move restlessly about inside the enclosure.

"He don't stand still for much more than a minute, if that," Hawthorn observed. "Did you hear him last night?"

"Hear him?"

"You were out like a light last night so I reckon you didn't. He was banging up against the corral like he was trying to tear it down around him, which is just exactly what he was trying to do, no doubt. But it held."

Sutton chuckled. "I'm glad to hear that. I don't take kindly to the idea of him busting loose and me having to chase after him all over again."

"They'll be writing you up in the record books," Hawthorn said, "as the man who was Wildfire's match."

"I'm not so sure I was a match for him. That horse has more brains, not to mention just plain guts, than most men I've known. I thought I had him at one point yesterday. I was hot on his heels and was getting ready to drop my loop on him when what does he do? He ups and changes direction on me so that instead of running straight on ahead of me, he turns to the left right in front of my face with the not-so-nice result that I ran straight into the herd and went tail over tin cup, me and my horse both."

Hawthorn laughed heartily.

Sutton assumed a wounded expression. "You wouldn't find it so funny if it had happened to you."

As Hawthorn's laughter faded away, he shook a finger at Sutton and said, "I warned you he was wily, didn't I?"

"You did. Trouble was I didn't know just how wily. I swear that fuzztail didn't make that turn by chance. I think he *planned* his move. Furthermore, I think he knew damn well that I'd collide with his herd and maybe kill myself."

"I'd say that's likely. I'd say anything's likely with that ton of horseflesh. You ought to hear some of the stories folk tell about him. They'd curl your hair."

"Watch it, Buck!" Sutton yelled and then pulled the older man away from the corral. "Here he comes!"

Wildfire charged the corral. Just before he reached it he leaped up into the air in an effort to escape. He knocked loose the top pole in one section of the enclosure but he failed in his bid for freedom. Sutton winced as the massive animal fell backward and hit the ground hard.

"Saints preserve us!" Hawthorn exclaimed. "Did you see that? Did you see the look in his eyes? Did you, Luke?"

"I did. I'd say that old horse looked just like the Devil red-hot from home."

"I'd best get up there and put that pole back in place," Hawthorn said, "else the next time he tries to be a bird and fly out of there he just might do it."

He went to the cabin and returned with a hammer and some nails. Sutton watched him scramble up the horizontal poles of the corral. Once at the top, Sutton handed him the pole Wildfire had dislodged and Hawthorn nailed it back into place.

On the ground again, Hawthorn, his gaze on the imprisoned horse restlessly prowling the inner perimeter of the corral, said, "Had me a stallion once that was a lot like him. Never did settle down once I had him penned. He tried the same trick as that one in there just did. He'd come a-running at the wall of the corral and leap into the air like he was as light as a feather. That's how he died—he died a-flying. One of the uprights was sticking up some and that stud, he didn't clear the top of the corral. He come down hard on that upright and skewered himself there. I had to shoot the critter to put him out of his misery."

"You think he'll try again to get out the way he just did?" Sutton asked uneasily.

"Sure, he will. At least, there's nothing he can stick himself on. But if he takes any more falls like the one he just did he's liable to break a leg or bust a gut and that'll be the end of him."

"Then I'd best get to bronc stomping. If I can knock some of the fight out of him there'll be a better than even chance that he won't end up harming himself. I'll go get my rope."

As Sutton started for the cabin, Hawthorn halted him with, "There's a rider coming."

Sutton turned and looked in the direction Hawthorn was pointing. He saw the lone rider in the distance and immediately thought of Judith Fletcher although the figure was too far away to tell whether it was a man or a woman.

"It's her," Hawthorn said a moment later as Sutton also recognized the rider as Judith. "By the way, I didn't mean to barge in on you two last night."

"No harm done."

Hawthorn gave Sutton a shrewd look. "Have you gone sweet on her? I mean that's what it looked like to me."

"She's a woman most any man would find it easy to like," Sutton answered and wondered why he was being evasive.

"Maybe she's come back to pick up where you two left off the last time you were together. So I'll be making myself scarce."

"There's no need for that, Buck. Stay. Maybe Judith has some news about her father and those would-be horse hunters you ought to hear."

But Sutton's words didn't stop Hawthorn, who continued on his way back to the cabin.

He had disappeared inside it by the time Judith rode up, drew rein, and dismounted. She stood without speaking, her eyes on Sutton. He was about to say something when she turned away from him, went up to the corral, and stood there watching the pacing Wildfire.

"You did it," she said softly after a long moment of silence. "You captured him."

Sutton joined her at the corral.

"He hates being locked up in there," Judith continued. "You can see that by the look in his eyes. In the way he moves—that stilted, almost lame way of walking he has."

"That's probably due to the fact that I had to tie his right hind leg to keep him from running off on the way back here."

"You tied him up?" Judith gave Sutton a quick glance before returning her attention to Wildfire.

He explained to her what he had done, concluding with, "It's an old trick mustangers—some of us—use to keep the horses we catch from getting away from us until we can pen them up."

"It's cruel."

"I can't deny that. Fact is though, I don't know any way to slow a horse down that's likely to run off that's not cruel to one degree or another. Take the way some Indian mustangers do it. They're partial to nailing heavy tar paper or shingles to a horse's hoof. Once they've done that, a horse has to step high to walk and that gets real tiring. What's more, it won't let him run at all.

"A worse way is the whip chain. A lot of mustangers use it though. They hook a two-foot chain to a leather band and then they fasten the band around one of the front legs of a wild horse. It gives the horse freedom of movement—so long as he walks or trots. But should he take on a faster gait, the chain whipsaws his front legs and keeps doing it till he catches on and goes back to walking."

"It's impossible not to admire man's ingenuity when it comes to creating methods of torture to use on beasts —or each other."

Sutton heard the sarcasm and bitterness in Judith's voice, which made him decide not to pursue the subject, not to tell her about the way he and Buck had brought back the mares they had captured—about the stuffing of those horses' nostrils to shorten their breath and thereby keep them from running away. Nor did he mention how he had cut a ligament in the legs of some of the mustangs to temporarily cripple them. She would no doubt find that practice cruel as well, if not barbaric. The less said at this point, he thought, the better. I've probably already said too much. He could feel her drawing away from him although she hadn't moved. There was a coldness to her voice and a rigidity to her stance that made her seem untouchable. And yet he wanted to touch her, wanted to hold her again in his arms as he had held her the night she arrived at the cabin to warn him about the wild horse hunt.

He reached out and turned her toward him. Looking into her eyes, searching them for some small sign of warmth, if not tenderness, he said, "The other night—"

He got no farther. Judith drew away from him and stepped back. "I don't want to talk about the other night."

"I do, Judith. I not only want to talk about it, I also want to remember it. I hope there will be other nights like it. Nights even better for both of us."

"Luke, I'm sorry. The other night—I know now that it was a mistake."

"Judith, it wasn't a mistake."

She sighed and withdrew from him. Speaking then in a strained voice, she said, "I was attracted to you. I'll admit that. I was, I believe, attracted to you from the first moment we met. There was something about you, something free and wild and strong. I remember thinking that you were like Wildfire in those respects. I remember thinking how much alike you and that stallion were."

"I don't know what to say, Judith."

"There is nothing to say. Not now that I see I was right about you. It would take a man like you to capture Wildfire. Someone as wild and as daring as he is. As clever. But I'm sorry to learn that you can also be cruel."

Sutton searched his mind for a way to change her feelings, for a way to make her understand that he had been acting in the best interests of Wildfire. He found

an apology on the tip of his tongue. But he could not—
would not—let himself utter it.

"You told me," Judith continued in the same
strained voice, "that you had been imprisoned and that
while you were imprisoned you learned to value the
freedom you had lost. Then how can you imprison
him?"

Sutton glanced at Wildfire as the stallion continued
to patrol the perimeter of the corral. "I had to if I was
to see to it that he got a better life. I told you why I
was after him the first day we met."

Judith gave him a scornful glance.

"I thought I had convinced you that he'll be a whole
lot better off back East."

"You did convince me at the time. But now, seeing
him like this, I've changed my mind again. I think I
was right in my original belief that he should remain
free. In fact, seeing him here like this and learning of
the suffering you've caused him so far—not to mention
what you'll do to him when you try to break him—I
just can't bear to think about it."

When Sutton said nothing, Judith continued.
"When I came here today I came hoping you had
failed to capture Wildfire. But somehow I knew you
had. Somehow I knew he would be no match for a man
like you."

Ordinarily Sutton would have taken Judith's last
statement as a compliment. But, based on the other
things she had just said about him, he was not all that
sure that she had meant it as a compliment.

A movement he caught out of the corner of his eye
caused him to turn his head. As he did so he saw Wildfire readying himself to make another run and leap
which might, this time, take him over the top of the
corral.

"Get back!" he yelled.

When Judith, seemingly mesmerized by the stallion as it began its run toward them, didn't move, he seized her roughly by the arm and pulled her backward.

She cried out in alarm and almost fell. Sutton held her upright as inside the corral Wildfire leaped high into the air—but not high enough to accomplish his purpose. His brisket struck the upper pole of the corral as his front legs penetrated the space between the two uppermost poles. They creaked with the force of the collision but did not break.

Judith cried out again—this time in shock—as Wildfire fell backward. "He's hurt himself!" she cried, pointing to the wounds on the stallion's brisket from which blood had begun to flow.

She turned her head, burying her face in her hands, and leaned weakly against Sutton.

He hesitated a moment and then his arms enfolded her and he began to hope that—

She pulled away from him, uncovering her face as she did so. She turned and looked at Wildfire who had gotten to his feet and was standing, apparently dazed, with bright lines of blood running down his brisket.

"He'll kill himself trying to get out of there!" she moaned. Spinning around so that she was once again facing Sutton, she exclaimed, "It's your fault! If he dies, it will be your fault and yours alone! You will have killed him by what you've done to him!"

She ran from Sutton then and in less than a minute was aboard her horse and riding away.

Sutton stood watching her rapid retreat. When she had finally disappeared from sight, he turned and went back to the cabin.

Hawthorn greeted him with, "Saw you two through

the window and you didn't look one bit like the love-birds you did the other night. What happened?"

"Judith thinks I mistreated Wildfire."

"How's that?"

"I told her how I tied up his leg to get him back here safe and sound. She doesn't like seeing him corraled, nor does she, I reckon, like the idea that I'm planning on busting him."

"Why, Lord a-mighty, bronc stomping is what a mustanger *does!*" a mystified Hawthorn exclaimed.

"I know that, Buck, the same as you do. But Judith, well, she's soft-hearted."

Hawthorn shook his head and muttered something unintelligible.

"Do you by any chance have a quirt I can borrow, Buck?"

"You're fixing to bust him now, are you?" Hawthorn asked, taking a quirt out of a cabinet drawer and handing it to Sutton.

"I am."

"Want some help?"

"I could use some, Buck, and that's a fact I'll be the first man to admit. What I've got penned up out there is no run-of-the-mill piece of horseflesh."

"Don't I know it though? He's a rip-roarer if ever there was one. I'll be glad to haze him for you."

Hawthorn bent down and picked up the battered saddle he had previously loaned to Sutton and handed it over. "You'll need these too," he said as he took down a mecate from a peg on the wall and picked up a length of cloth that was lying on the dusty windowsill. He handed them both to Sutton and the two men made their way outside where Sutton headed for the corral and Hawthorn headed for his horse. Sutton stood with one boot heel hooked on a corral pole and

watched Wildfire, until he was joined by Hawthorn,
who rode up aboard his horse a few minutes later.

"I'm ready if you are," he announced.

Sutton opened the corral gate and Hawthorn,
swinging a wide loop, rode into the corral. Sutton,
right behind him, closed the corral gate.

Wildfire backed away from the advancing Hawthorn. The stallion began to nicker and to prance nervously about.

Hawthorn missed on his first try to lasso the horse
because Wildfire had seen the rope coming and moved
swiftly out of its way.

"This critter can read my mind," Hawthorn com-
plained loudly as he reeled his rope in and got ready to
try again.

Wildfire began to run around the inside of the corral
at a fairly fast pace. Unruffled, Hawthorn at first
turned his horse on the spot where it stood, whirling
his loop in the air above his head. But then, as Wildfire
continued his evasive tactic, Hawthorn simply held his
mount in position and let the stallion run in a circle
until he reappeared again in front of the patient mustanger. This time when Hawthorn let his rope go, it
sailed smoothly through the air and the dust Wildfire
was raising to land neatly around its target's neck.

Hawthorn rode up to Wildfire, running up the rope
and taking dallies around his saddle horn as he swiftly
shortened the distance between himself and the horse.

Wildfire fought the rope but to no avail. Within
minutes Hawthorn had the mustang's nose pressed
against the horn on his saddle.

"He's all yours now, Luke!" he yelled.

Sutton moved toward the mustang, staying well out
of range of Wildfire's legs. When he was standing next
to the horse, he slipped the mecate over the animal's

head. When he had it firmly in place, he used the cloth Hawthorn had given him to blindfold the straining horse.

"I'll keep him eared down good while you saddle up, Luke."

Sutton slapped Hawthorn's saddle on Wildfire's back. The instant he did so the horse kicked out with his hind legs in dumb protest. Sutton ignored the move and concentrated on fastening the saddle in place. When he had done so, he exchanged glances with Hawthorn; then, putting a foot in a stirrup, he swung aboard Wildfire and took a deep seat. He got a firm grip on the double-reined mecate with his left hand and, with the rawhide quirt held tightly in his right hand, he yelled, "Turn him loose, Buck!"

Hawthorn removed his rope from Wildfire's neck and then removed the blindfold from the animal's eyes. When he had done so he backed his horse away to give Sutton room.

Wildfire stood stiff-legged and blinking in the sunlight.

Sutton clucked to him. When he received no immediate response, he dug his heels into the animal's flanks and quirted the horse.

Wildfire exploded.

The stallion jumped four times in quick succession, and each of his four landings sent shock waves through Sutton's body. Wildfire whirled in a semicircle and then proceeded to whirl wildly in the opposite direction. Sutton held tightly to the mecate with his right hand while simultaneously gripping a fistful of the mustang's mane with his left.

Wildfire kicked backward, seeming to stand on his head for a moment. Then he reared, supporting himself on his hind legs, his front legs wildly slashing the air. As his front hooves hit the ground a moment later, he gave a violent shake of his entire body, then another one equally violent, as he struggled to unseat Sutton.

But Sutton would not be unseated, although he did leave the saddle a few times. At such times, when his buttocks bounced back into the saddle, his teeth chattered as a result of the jarring he received.

Wildfire suddenly bunched his four feet under him. He lowered his back and then abruptly arched it.

Sutton flew up into the air for a distance of nearly three feet. He came down onto the saddle again with a tremendous jolt. But he had no time to recover because Wildfire immediately repeated his maneuver. This time when Sutton came down, he was almost thrown from the saddle but he managed to keep his seat. He let go of the mustang's mane and then seized the horse's left ear, which he twisted first one way and then the other.

Wildfire swung his head around in order to bite Sutton's leg but he was unable to do so. Sutton twisted the animal's ear a second time. This time Wildfire reacted by racing toward the corral's wall. When he reached it, he rubbed up against the poles in an attempt to scrape Sutton from his back. But, because Sutton had known what the horse was up to the minute it began to run, he had swung his right leg up and over the saddle horn with the result that Wildfire succeeded in scraping only his own hide.

"Hold tight, Luke!" Hawthorn yelled through hands he had cupped around his mouth. "If the sonofabitch throws you, he'll stomp you so far down into the ground you'll take root and sprout!"

"Open the gate, Buck. It's high time I gave this gut-twister something else to occupy his mind."

When Hawthorn had opened the gate and ridden

out of the corral, Sutton turned Wildfire so that he could see the open gate. The horse made for it at a bone-snapping pace. Once through it, he headed away from the corral at a gallop.

Sutton gripped the mecate with both hands and the horse with both legs. He had taken the latter action in part to cut down on the animal's wind, and thus slow him down, as well as to help himself stay in the saddle.

But even with his lungs constricted somewhat by the pressure Sutton's legs were exerting, Wildfire did not slow down. It seemed to Sutton that he ran even faster. Sutton held on, determined to ride the horse until it dropped—or until he was thrown. But he didn't expect to be thrown, not with Wildfire running as if a score of demons were on his trail; the mustang had no time to buck now.

The ride became a test of endurance for both horse and man. Neither of them showed any sign of quitting. Wildfire ran doggedly on. Sometimes he veered one way or the other. Occasionally a shudder would run through his body. Sweat coated him as it did Sutton's face and body.

Sutton had no clear idea how much time had passed —it had begun to seem that he had been aboard Wildfire for an eternity or, if not that long, at least since the day he was born—but finally the horse slowed his killing pace, came to a gradual halt, and stood as stiff-legged as he had the moment Hawthorn had removed the blindfold from his eyes, back in the corral.

Sutton braced himself, readying himself for the animal's next move while trying to guess what it would be and when it would come.

Wildfire made no move. He continued to stand with his head hanging down, the sweat dripping from his body.

"You've done it, Luke!" Hawthorn crowed as he rode up and drew rein next to Sutton. "You've roughed him out for sure!"

Sutton wasn't nearly so sure. Not until Hawthorn had begun to haze the stallion back toward the corral, and Wildfire—obviously exhausted and carrying his tail limply between his legs—meekly submitted to the hazing without making even a feeble attempt to unseat his rider, did he let himself begin to believe that he had tamed the hurricane men called Wildfire.

That afternoon, as he had planned, he returned to the corral carrying his own gear. As he approached, Wildfire shied from him at first but then allowed him to place a saddle blanket on his back. He fought the bit and the bridle however and, in order to get them on the stallion, Sutton was forced to twist the animal's ear until he submitted to the process.

He also fought the saddle but with less energy. When Sutton had cinched it in place and flipped down his stirrups, he swung into the saddle. When Wildfire did not react, Sutton, using both hands on the reins as was his custom when training a horse, proceeded to teach Wildfire to turn. He did this by holding both reins in his right hand and letting his left hand slide down the left rein as far as necessary to turn the horse to the left. He repeated the process numerous times until only the slightest touch of his hand on the left rein was enough to turn the stallion. Satisfied, he reversed the process, and Wildfire, he was pleased to see, quickly learned to turn to the right with only slight pressure on the right rein.

He spent the next hour bending Wildfire away from the poles of the corral because the horse had a tendency to hug them, turning the horse by neck-reining, and reinforcing lateral control.

Walking the horse over to the corral gate, he leaned down and opened it. Wildfire, as the gate swung open, went through it at a fast gallop. Sutton let the animal run, knowing that the mustang was instinctively seeking freedom, and knowing too that he could, he was almost certain, curb the animal when the time came to do so. Such proved to be the case. Several minutes later, when he drew rein, Wildfire slowed and then stopped without fighting the bit.

Sutton spent some time after that sharpening Wildfire's responses to the reins and using his legs in a slight bumping fashion to give an easy rhythm to each turn. He kept at it until the sun was easing down toward the horizon, sometimes talking to Wildfire, sometimes simply humming to the horse, occasionally patting the animal's neck to show his pleasure at the way the lessons were being learned.

When he returned to the cabin carrying his gear that evening, he found Hawthorn standing outside it.

"You've got that bronc out there in the corral acting like he was born with a saddle on his back and a bit in his mouth," the admiring mustanger observed.

Sutton grinned.

"I reckon you'll be leaving pretty soon now that you've done what you came out here to do."

"I'll be heading out tomorrow, Buck."

"I kind of hate to see you go. It gets lonesome out here in the hills. Having you around's been kind of a comfort. It's been a long time since I had somebody I could talk to." Hawthorn paused a moment and then: "I've been thinking, Luke."

Sutton waited.

"I've been thinking," Hawthorn continued, "that maybe I could pay you a monthly salary to stay here and help me stomp broncs. The salary, it'd be on top of meals and lodging, such as they are, of course."

"I thank you for the offer, Buck. An offer like that coming from a real professional bronc buster like yourself—it makes me proud that you think enough of me to make it."

"Then you'll do it? You'll stay on here?"

Sutton shook his head. "I've got to take Wildfire back to Virginia City and turn him over to Mr. Wilson, who's waiting on me back there."

"Fine. When you've done that, you can come back here."

"Buck, I don't want you to think I don't appreciate your offer. I do. But the fact is, I'm just not cut out to be a mustanger anymore. I wouldn't've been doing it here with you were it not for Mr. Wilson hiring me to hunt down and break this here horse."

"To tell you the truth," Hawthorn said, "I didn't think you'd take me up on my offer. But I wanted to make it just in case it might turn out to appeal to you."

That night as Sutton slept, something penetrated his consciousness, something disturbing that disrupted his sleep. He turned over and pulled his blanket up around his neck as he tried to go back to sleep. But he remained conscious, although groggy. As he shifted position on his bunk, he heard a sound and sat up in bed, his blanket falling away from him.

Wildfire!

He was sure he had heard the horse nicker. He sat there listening. At first he heard nothing more. Then the nicker came again, louder this time. He dismissed the sound as nothing important and was about to lie back down again when a second different sound reached his ears: the sound of wood creaking.

Maybe, he thought, that stud's trying to break out of the corral again. He swung his legs over the side of the bunk, quickly pulled on his jeans and then his boots. He went over to the open window and peered out into the night. A startled grunt burst from his lips when he saw Judith Fletcher moving about in the moonlight as she opened and swung back the gate of the corral.

"Hey!" he yelled through the window. *"Shut that gate!"*

He ran for the door, threw it open, and dashed outside.

But he was too late.

Wildfire sped out of the corral and went galloping away.

Sutton turned and ran for his horse, intending to go after the stallion. But before he reached his black, Judith Fletcher called out, "Stay where you are!"

When he glanced back over his shoulder, he saw the cocked six-shooter in her hand, aimed directly at him.

TEN

SUTTON TURNED AROUND to face Judith, his eyes on her and not on the gun in her hand. He took a step toward her.

"Stop!"

He didn't. He took another step and then another, his eyes still on her face. "You won't shoot me," he told her.

"I will if you take one more step. I swear I will."

But, as Sutton continued moving closer to her, she didn't shoot. The gun in her hand began to waver. When he was only a few feet away from her, she lowered both the gun and her eyes.

Sutton stepped up to her and put his hands on her shoulders. "Why'd you do it?" he asked her.

When she did not answer, he tilted her chin so that she was looking up at him. He repeated his question.

She told him then what he already knew she would tell him, even before he had asked his question. She spoke of freedom and about how certain creatures were not meant to be penned up. She told him how she had brooded since parting from him yesterday, and how she had lain awake most of the night thinking about Wildfire. She told him how she had finally made up her mind to free the stallion, and how she had brought with her one of her father's guns in case Sutton or Hawthorn or both of them tried to stop her from doing what she had decided she must do.

"You made a big mistake, missy."

Sutton turned to find Hawthorn standing behind him.

"I heard what you just told Luke," the mustanger said. "I reckon I can understand how you felt about that stallion, but what I damn well can't understand is why you turned him loose so he could get himself killed by some wild horse hunter."

"He won't be killed," Judith argued. "He's survived before. He will continue to do so."

"Maybe. More likely not. Some stud killer'll get him, you mark my words."

"None of them have succeeded in doing so yet," Judith stubbornly pointed out.

"That's not because they ain't all tried," Hawthorn countered. "When your pa and Mel Dunbar and those other boys was out hunting Wildfire the other day, I led them astray so's Luke here would have a fair chance to catch that stallion. But I ain't going to be able to do that every time those fellows take a notion to go out wild horse hunting. As a matter of plain fact, they told me they was planning on taking a day off—which was yesterday, by the way—and then heading out again this morning after Wildfire. Only this time they've added a little spice to the hunt."

"What are you getting at, Buck?" Sutton inquired.

"I didn't bother mentioning it to you yesterday when you got back, Luke, on account of the whole thing seemed a moot matter since you'd just caught Wildfire. What I'm getting at is Abe Fletcher and Mel Dunbar between them have placed a bounty on Wildfire's head. A bounty amounting to a neat five hundred dollars which they'll pay, they say, to the man or men who can kill that stallion and show them his corpse."

"I didn't know that," Judith breathed. "Father never mentioned the bounty to me."

"That may well be on account of he knows you've got a soft spot in your heart for that horse," Hawthorn pointed out. "Maybe he didn't want to upset you by mentioning it. Anyways, you've gone and upset the applecart for sure now, missy, with what you just did on account of that soft spot you got in your heart—not to mention the one in your head."

"Five hundred dollars," Judith said in a low voice. "I've heard of men who would kill other *men* for that kind of money. Such men would surely not hesitate to kill a *horse* for it."

"You've hit the nail square on the head, missy," Hawthorn said dolefully.

"Oh, Luke," Judith cried, "what have I done?"

It was Hawthorn who answered her question. "What you've done is gone and signed Wildfire's death warrant, like as not."

"That's not necessarily so," Sutton contradicted. "Not if I can catch Wildfire all over again, it's not."

"Do you think you can, Luke?" Judith asked anxiously.

"He's the man that can if any man can," Hawthorn said decisively. "And I'm the man to help him do it."

"I'll go get the rest of my clothes," Sutton said, "and then we can ride out after Wildfire, Buck."

"I'll go with you and Mr. Hawthorn, Luke," Judith said.

"You had best go home," Hawthorn advised sternly, "and try to stay out of any more mischief, missy."

"But I may be of some help to you."

"What kind of help could you be on a wild horse hunt?" Hawthorn asked Judith skeptically.

"I could—oh, I don't know what I could do," she

replied. "But I want to go with you and try to undo what I've done if that's possible."

Before Hawthorn could say any more, Sutton said, "You're in for some rough riding if you try to keep up with us, Judith. Do you want to let yourself in for that?"

Judith nodded. "I was riding horses before I could walk. I may be a foolish woman. But I am not a helpless one. I'll ride with you."

The trio reached Pole Creek just before dawn. By late morning they had reached Brewster's Rest. At the stage station, they halted and Sutton went inside to ask Brewster if he had seen any wild horses in the area.

"Sure, I have," was Brewster's answer. "They're around here all the time. They cause me no end of trouble. They make any mares the stage line uses frisky as snowflakes in a big wind. Runs them off, the stallions do, and that causes one heap of headaches for everybody concerned. Slows the stage. Passengers fret and complain about the delays. Drivers—"

"I'm interested in one particular horse—a stallion folks call Wildfire."

"Aha! You're out hunting him too, are you?"

"What do you mean, 'too'?"

"Heard about the bounty some ranchers down south are ready to pay anybody who can kill him. Five hundred dollars it is, I heard. You out to collect it, are you?"

Sutton didn't bother to answer the question. "Did somebody else come by your place looking to collect the bounty? Is that why you said 'too'?"

"Yup. Fellow said his name was Stoner. Nothing more—just Stoner."

"What did you tell him?"

"The same thing I told you just now. Namely, that there's always a lot of loose broncs running round about these parts. But I told him I hadn't seen Wildfire lately. So maybe he's took off for greener pastures."

"Which way was Stoner headed, did he say?"

"Over toward White Pine County. He said a fellow he'd met back along the trail told him Wildfire was partial to a canyon over that way near the county line. It's due east of here about ten miles or so—where him and his mares like to hide from folks like yourself who are out hunting him and his herd."

"How long ago did Stoner leave here?"

"Close to an hour ago. He got an early start same as yourself."

"I'm obliged to you."

Outside again, Sutton told Hawthorn and Judith what he had just learned, concluding with a question for Judith. "I take it you never told your father about me catching Wildfire."

"No, I didn't. I didn't see Father yesterday at all. He was out on the range all day. Why do you ask?"

"It figures," Sutton mused. "When I was listening to what Brewster had to say just now about Wildfire, it struck me that Stoner wouldn't be out there hunting the stallion if he'd known that I already had him corraled."

"Is he very far ahead of us?" Hawthorn asked.

"Stoner was here about an hour ago," Sutton answered. "But he doesn't know any more about Wildfire than we do. There's a good chance that Wildfire might not be in that canyon Stoner found out about."

"Do you think Wildfire's back with his herd?" Hawthorn asked.

"Don't know," Sutton answered. "He might not have rejoined the herd. He might be content to be on his own for a spell. Maybe he'll try to start himself another harem."

"But you think we should go and take a look at that canyon," Judith said.

"I do," Sutton said as he climbed back into the saddle.

They moved out, circled Brewster's Rest, and rode in an easterly direction.

"I have a suggestion," Judith said before they had gone very far. "If we stay together we have one chance of finding Wildfire. But if we separate we have three chances. That is, each one of us has a chance to find him."

"If you found him, could you catch him?" Hawthorn asked her derisively.

"No, of course not," Judith admitted. "But I could rejoin Luke and tell him where I'd seen Wildfire."

"I think your idea's a good one," Sutton told Judith. "Buck, you ride north from here, and Judith you ride south. Both of you can scout the countryside for any sign of Wildfire and then meet me east of where we're at now, at the canyon Brewster said Stoner was heading for."

"In a way," Judith said thoughtfully, "I hope Wildfire isn't in the canyon, with or without his herd."

Sutton knew the basis for her hope. Since Stoner had a good head start on them, he could easily kill Wildfire in the canyon, if that's where the stallion was, long before Sutton or the others could get there to stop him.

"Give yourselves about an hour," he told Hawthorn and Judith. "Then meet me at the canyon. I'll wait there for you or, if it turns out that either of you two get there first, you wait for me to show up."

Sutton dug his heels into his black and went gallop-

ing eastward, a mocking image of the stud killer
Stoner haunting his mind along with the sound of
Stoner's deadly gunfire.

When he was sure he had covered two miles, he began
to search the area for the canyon Brewster had mentioned. The countryside around him was rugged,
dotted with valleys that slumbered between sharp-
peaked mountains and lower hills, which made the
search difficult. But he persevered, riding up one slope
and then down another, having seen no sign of a canyon from the crest he had reached, knowing he must
keep on trying to find it before . . . He did not let
himself complete the thought but concentrated instead
on the search, consoling himself with the thought that
Wildfire might not have taken refuge in the elusive
canyon.

Nearly an hour passed and he still had not found the
canyon nor had he seen any sign of wild horses in the
vicinity. He was on the verge of giving up the search,
beginning to believe that he had either passed the canyon or that it must lay somewhere ahead of him, when
he heard the whiplike whine of a rifle shot.

Stoner, he thought, as the sound drew him and he
rode rapidly east through a stand of stunted cotton-
woods bordering a shallow creek. Or somebody as bad,
if not worse. Wildfire, he thought, and slammed his
heels into his horse.

The chilling sound of a second rifle shot caused him
to change direction. He headed northeast. As he
topped a rise, he saw the horse—Stoner's mount,
which he had seen once before—down in the valley
below. But he saw no sign of Stoner himself. He rode
down the rise. Once on relatively level ground again,

he headed toward Stoner's horse, which watched him approach.

Before he reached it, the horse tossed its head and went trotting away from him. Moments later, it disappeared from sight. Sutton followed it—and found the narrow mouth of a canyon which was half hidden by towering pines, and into which Stoner's horse had wandered. He knew instantly that it was the canyon Brewster had told him about, because it was full of mustangs milling nervously, some of them heading toward the mouth of the canyon.

Sutton stood up in his stirrups, searching. Wildfire was at the far end of the canyon, standing on a tall rocky ledge so that he could survey the scene with ease. Sutton looked up as Wildfire was doing and saw Stoner perched on the rim of the canyon's wall.

He pulled his rifle from his saddle boot and shouldered it. Sighting carefully, he fired a warning shot over Stoner's head. The stocky stud killer responded by ducking down fast and then gingerly raising his head and peering down at Sutton.

"He's mine!" Sutton yelled up to the man.

Stoner's contemptuous laughter drifted down to Sutton.

As Stoner's rifle reappeared and he took aim at Wildfire, Sutton was about to fire another warning shot, one that he vowed would come close enough to raise the hair on Stoner's neck.

But, before either man could fire, Wildfire screamed a warning and his herd, alerted and alarmed by the sound, began to flee from the canyon.

Sutton slammed his rifle back into the boot, swiftly turned his horse, and galloped away from the canyon's entrance to avoid being trampled to death by the onrushing herd.

He took up a safe position to the left of the canyon's entrance and sat his saddle there as the first of the herd, led by the white mare that usually led them, came careening out of the narrow entrance. Sutton winced as the sound of another shot echoed briefly inside the canyon before fading beneath the overpowering sound of pounding hooves.

He watched as the horses emerged from the canyon, hoping to catch sight of Wildfire. Seeing no sign of the stallion, his body stiffened and his mouth went dry.

He'll be bringing up the rear like always, he assured himself. The fact that I can't see him don't mean he's dead. He swore at the pace of the exodus from the canyon, which was agonizingly slow because no more than two horses could pass through the entrance at one time. He braced himself for another of Stoner's shots but none came. Even so, he was unable to relax.

The minutes passed, stretching, it began to seem to Sutton, into an eternity. Dust filled the air, stirred up by the fleeing mustangs, Stoner's saddled mount among them.

Sutton continued to wait, his rope in his hand now, his legs gripping his black as he made ready for the blood-boiling chase he hoped was coming—if Stoner had not succeeded in killing Wildfire. Horse after horse, some of them running in pairs, flew past him and away. He never once took his eyes from the canyon's entrance as he waited for Wildfire, hoping desperately that the mustang was still alive.

Somehow, the thought of Wildfire going down with Stoner's bullet—or bullets—in him struck Sutton as obscene. To kill the horse for five hundred dollars—or for twice or even thrice that amount—seemed to him to be a savage act of senseless destruction done for the very basest of motives. Hatred for Stoner flooded him.

That hatred grew still greater when no more horses galloped out of the canyon. He walked his black toward the entrance, intending to enter the canyon and see for himself if Wildfire had indeed been killed. But, before his horse had taken more than a few steps, Wildfire burst like a bullet from the canyon.

Sutton, elated at the sight of the stallion, started after him the moment the mustang sped past him. As he did so he saw Stoner scrambling down the side of the canyon, his rifle still in his hands. As the stud killer got down on one knee and brought the stock of his rifle smartly up against his shoulder to take aim at Wildfire, Sutton swore. His revolver cleared leather and he went galloping back toward Stoner. He got off a fast snapshot that hit the barrel of Stoner's rifle, which he had aimed at, knocking the gun to one side. He saw Stoner's lips move but he couldn't hear the man's words because of the pounding sound made by the fleeing Wildfire's hooves.

As Stoner swung his rifle back into position and took aim at the escaping horse, Sutton was almost upon him. He did not fire again but instead threw himself from the saddle. He landed on top of Stoner and brought the man down to the ground. Stoner's rifle fired but the round did no more damage than to rip a thin limb from a nearby tree.

Sutton seized the gun's warm barrel and, with one knee pressing down hard on Stoner's chest, wrested the weapon from the man's hands and threw it to one side. Stoner clawed frantically at Sutton's face, cursing vehemently all the while, as he tried to knee Sutton in the groin. Sutton got off him, hauled him to his feet, and, clutching a fistful of the man's shirt in his left hand, slammed him back against the canyon's rocky wall.

"I told you," Sutton muttered through clenched teeth, "that stud's mine and nobody else's."

"He no more belongs to you than the moon does," Stoner snapped, his hands tearing at Sutton's which were still pressing him back against the canyon wall. "Your brand's not on him."

"That may be," Sutton admitted, "but he's still mine. You want to know why he is? Because I say so and because I'm a man who can back up what he says with his fists or his gun if that's what it takes. Now, I want you out of here, Stoner. I want you out of here right now. Your horse—you see it over there where it broke free of the herd? Good. Well, you go get on it and ride on out of here and don't you come back after Wildfire or I might have to kill you to prove to you that I mean what I say."

Stoner swung as Sutton released him. Sutton blocked the blow with a raised forearm and then gave Stoner a hard left jab that left the stud killer bending over and breathless. Flipping his six-gun from his right to his left hand, Sutton swung a right that caught Stoner on the left side of his jaw, snapping the man's head back.

Stoner dropped to his knees. He looked up at Sutton and then began to crawl toward the spot where his rifle lay on the ground.

Sutton stepped in front of him. "Leave that gun where it is, Stoner. I don't trust you. You'd come back here the minute my back was turned and this time, on account of all the bad blood that's between us, you just might take a notion to kill Wildfire *and* me. Get up now and get going!"

Stoner struggled to his feet. Glaring at Sutton over his shoulder, he staggered toward his horse. As he started to climb into the saddle, Sutton turned away from him and was astonished to see Wildfire standing almost motionless twenty yards away.

Suddenly, Sutton caught a flicker of movement out of the corner of his eye. He turned quickly, saw Stoner rip a knife from the necklace of dirty twine he wore around his neck beneath his shirt. Before the stud killer could throw the knife, Sutton fired and the trigger finger flew from Stoner's suddenly bloody right hand.

As Stoner's knife fell from his hand, Sutton, blowing smoke away from the uptilted barrel of his gun, said mockingly, "I fired that shot with my left hand, Stoner. I would have taken off your whole hand and not just one finger had I had my gun in my right hand. Now, I've heard it said that a word to the wise is sufficient. Are you a wise man, Stoner?"

Stoner's silent answer to the mocking question was a quick climb into the saddle and an even quicker departure from the scene.

Sutton didn't move for several minutes but remained standing where he was, watching and listening. When he was satisfied that Stoner was indeed gone and no longer a threat to him or to Wildfire, he turned back to gaze again at the stallion that was still standing where he had last seen it.

He eased over to his black and removed his rope from the saddle horn. He began to fashion a loop, keeping his movements to a bare minimum because he did not want to spook Wildfire and start the stallion running again. But the horse did not move, not even when Sutton climbed into the saddle and walked his mount in Wildfire's direction. He fully expected the stallion to turn and make a run for it at any moment. He was prepared for such a move. The minute the mustang made it he intended to let his loop fly.

But the mustang remained where he was, tossing his head and staring straight at Sutton. Occasionally he pawed the ground with a hoof, stirring up dust devils that danced briefly in the breeze before dying.

"What's wrong, old fellow?" Sutton asked softly as he came close to the stallion. "Aren't you ready to go chasing after your ladies?"

Wildfire arched his neck and looked away from Sutton.

"They ran off and left you in the lurch. But I haven't. I came looking for you right after you ran off from me. How come you're not running now?"

He thought he knew the answer to his question and yet he couldn't quite bring himself to believe the answer was a true one. It went against everything—or almost everything—he had learned about wild horses during his days as a mustanger. They fought you tooth and nail and every inch of the way. Some of them, even after having been broken, still wouldn't tolerate the touch of a saddle or bridle without putting up a fight.

But there was more—at least there was more where Wildfire was concerned. Sutton recalled the words he had heard people use to describe the stallion. Elusive. Wily. Intelligent. It was that last word that embodied the difference that set Wildfire apart from other mustangs he had known. It explained, he believed, why the stallion had not fled.

He knows, Sutton thought. Damn if he don't! He knows I didn't show up here to do him harm like Stoner did. Somehow or other he knows the difference between the two of us. What's more, he knows I shot at Stoner to try to save his life if I could.

He dismounted. He stood beside his horse for a long moment, his rope hanging loosely in his right hand.

Then he moved slowly in Wildfire's direction, talking softly as he went, telling the stallion that he wouldn't let any harm come to him, whispering that everything was going to be fine, assuring the animal that he had a good life waiting for him back East and that, though his world was about to change and change radically, he would have no cause to regret the change.

"Oh, maybe you'll wake up sometime and remember a dream you were having about the open range and you'll start wondering where your ladies are. But then you'll start forgetting about those things because Mr. Wilson, he'll keep you fat and sassy. He'll pay men to groom you, feed and exercise you, introduce you to some high-toned Eastern ladies—why, you won't want for a thing.

"They've got no cougars back East that'll drop down out of a tree on you and start tearing you apart while you're still alive and kicking. You won't starve when Nevada's winters turn the whole world white and there's not a blade of grass to graze or a bit of forage to be found anywhere and you wind up starving to death long before the snow melts and spring comes."

He was only a few feet from the horse now. Wildfire nickered. He moved still closer to him. He shifted the rope to his left hand. His right hand rose and reached out. It came to rest on Wildfire's shoulder. The horse flinched. He felt the heat of the animal's body beneath his hand. He stroked the stallion's shoulder and then ran his hand through Wildfire's tangled mane. He held up the rope, touched the horse's neck with it, said that it wouldn't hurt him, he'd be sure to see to that, asked Wildfire if he was ready to go, and only then remembered that he had said he would wait here for Judith and Hawthorn to join him.

"We'll wait here for a spell," he said. "Then we'll go,

you and me." He stepped back, his hand wet from the sweat soaking Wildfire's body. "I reckon you're thirsty after all the running you did. I've got water." He went back to his black where he took off his hat, turned it upside down, and emptied some of the water in his canteen into it. He returned to Wildfire and, holding his hat in both hands, held it out to the horse.

As the stallion drank, Sutton said, "I took this job in the first place to earn myself some money—some good money. But I'll tell you a secret. From the minute I first laid eyes on you, it wasn't the money I was after. It was keeping you alive that was uppermost in my mind. And, by golly, I did do that, didn't I?"

Wildfire raised his head, shook it, and droplets of water flew in every direction, some of them wetting Sutton's face.

He returned to his black, keeping one eye on Wildfire, and proceeded to strip his gear from it. Then he returned to Wildfire, carrying his gear slung over his shoulder. Working slowly and speaking all the time in a soft voice to the mustang, he proceeded to saddle and bridle Wildfire. He was tightening his cinch strap when he heard the distant but unmistakable sound of gunfire.

Made uneasy by the noise and the message he believed it conveyed, he began to work faster. Straightening, he flipped down his stirrups. He waited a moment, stroking Wildfire's neck, aware that the horse now no longer automatically quivered at his touch. He let several minutes pass during which, he hoped, the stallion would become accustomed to the saddle and bridle. Then he stepped into the saddle and sat there, waiting to see what Wildfire would do.

The mustang did nothing. He did not bolt. He did not buck. He did not kick.

Sutton smiled. Picking up the reins, he turned Wildfire, first to the left, then to the right.

More gunfire, an ominous omen.

Sutton considered heading for safer surroundings. But he had promised to meet Judith and Hawthorn here and he did not want to leave without saying goodbye to them. He continued riding Wildfire for short distances, turning the horse to one side or the other, riding back, halting starting out again.

He drew rein when he saw someone riding toward him in the distance. Shielding his eyes from the sun by pulling his hat down low on his forehead, he squinted in the bright light and was soon able to make out the figure of Judith Fletcher as she came galloping toward him.

"Luke!" she called out when she was still some distance away.

As she rode up to join him, her eyes widened in apparent disbelief and she stared, not at Sutton, but at Wildfire. "That's not"—she turned and pointed—"*there's* your horse." Looking back at Wildfire and then up at Sutton, she marveled, "He's as gentle as a lamb. It's amazing. It's absolutely amazing."

Sutton smiled again. "Him and me," he said, patting the mustang's neck, "we get along just fine now."

"It would certainly seem so."

"Did you have any trouble finding the place?"

"No. I saw the tracks left by a wild horse herd coming from this direction and I followed them here. I thought they might have been Wildfire's herd. They were, weren't they?"

Sutton told Judith what had happened and how he had run off Stoner.

"I heard gunfire on my way here," Judith said when he had finished. "Maybe that was Stoner."

"It wasn't."

"How can you be sure?"

"That's Stoner's rifle lying over there on the ground where I made him leave it."

"What are you going to do now, Luke? Take Wildfire back to Mr. Hawthorn's cabin?"

"No, I'm not." Sutton got out of the saddle and went over to Judith. He helped her down from her horse.

"You're leaving," she said in a low voice.

Sutton took her in his arms. "If I ever get back this way, I'll come calling on you."

"I don't think I can wait for that to happen, Luke. It just occurred to me that I am in absolutely desperate need of some new clothes. A party dress. One or two nice day dresses. Some new shoes and stockings. Oh, I am in need of ever so many things."

"I'm not sure I follow you."

"There are several wonderful shops on D Street in Virginia City that I've been to on visits to the city. There is one that employs this lovely little old lady who is an absolute genius with fittings. I know what I shall do. I'll make arrangements to come to Virginia City to buy some new clothes. I can be there by the middle of next week. That's only a few days away. Will you be there to take me out on the town, Luke?"

Sutton's arms tightened their grip on Judith as he smiled down at her and said, "I most surely will be. That's a promise." He bent his head and their lips met.

Sometime later, they drew apart at the sound of a chuckle.

"I didn't hear you ride up, Buck," an embarrassed Sutton told a brightly blushing Hawthorn, who was sitting his saddle and staring down at the couple.

"I've no doubt you didn't hear me," Hawthorn said.

"Not with the way you two were going at it so hot and heavy."

"We were just—" Sutton began but Hawthorn interrupted him with, "I can see what you two were just. But I've more important matters on my mind at the moment. I ran into Fletcher, Dunbar, and a whole passel of riders who were with them. I told them I was on my way up to Palisade to buy some supplies. Told them too that I'd seen Wildfire and his harem heading east so as to keep them from coming this way.

"I also ran into some soldiers back along the trail. They're having themselves a field day shooting wild horses. I'm mighty glad to see that you caught Wildfire before either Fletcher and his boys or those trigger-quick soldiers happened to mosey this way. Luke, what's Wildfire standing there like that for—so meek and mild, I mean? Ain't you afraid he'll take off on you?"

Sutton shook his head. "Like I told Judith, Buck, the two of us are pals now. We get along together real good."

"Well, let's take him back to the cabin," Hawthorn suggested.

"I won't be going back to the cabin with you, Buck."

"You're heading home from here, are you?"

"I am."

"Well, I can't say I'm glad to see you go."

"I want to thank you for all you did for me, Buck, for all your help. By the way—you see that rifle lying over there on the ground? It belonged to Stoner. I had a run-in with him and he took off. You're welcome to his gun. He won't be back for it."

Hawthorn retrieved Stoner's rifle and then turned back to Sutton. "If you ever get another bad case of mustang fever, Luke, why, you know where to come to cure it."

"I do, Buck, I surely do."

Sutton shook hands with the mustanger and then whispered to Judith that she could find him at the International Hotel in Virginia City when she arrived there the following week.

Then he swung into the saddle and, driving his black before him, rode west. Looking back over his shoulder, he waved. Both Judith and Hawthorn returned his wave. But Judith did more; she blew him a kiss which, he was amused to see, caused Hawthorn to begin blushing all over again.

"He's even more impressive up close like this," Ronald Wilson said as he stood with Sutton outside Wildfire's stall in a livery barn in Virginia City. "Much more—what is the word I want? I know. Awesome. That's the best word to describe him."

"He is that," Sutton agreed.

"And you say you've broken him to the saddle?"

"I have. Let me show you."

After borrowing a saddle and bridle from the liveryman, Sutton got Wildfire ready to ride. Then, after leading the horse outside with Wilson following alongside, he swung into the saddle and walked the stallion down C Street. He returned at a trot which became a gallop. After drawing rein in front of the admiring Wilson, he dismounted and handed Wildfire's reins to the man.

"Violet assured me," Wilson said, "just before she and Aaron left on their honeymoon that you would bring him back, Luke; but I must confess I had some doubts about that, despite Violet's assurances that you were both intrepid and resourceful and that if any mustanger could capture Wildfire it was you. I am happy to see that my daughter was right in having such strong faith in you."

"Would you like to ride Wildfire yourself?" Sutton asked.

"I would be happy to. If you'll excuse me, Luke . . ."

Sutton stood aside and watched as Wilson stepped gracefully into the saddle, and knew at once that he was watching a highly skilled horseman.

Wilson stroked the stallion's neck and talked to him in a soothing voice. Wildfire moved forward with an assured step. Sutton continued watching admiringly as Wilson put him first to a lope, then pulled him back to a brisk walk, and finally wheeled him around in one direction, then in the opposite direction.

By the time Wilson had returned to where Sutton awaited him, he was beaming. He dismounted and clapped Sutton on the back. "You've done it, Luke, no doubt about it. You've tamed this magnificent creature to a fare-thee-well."

He led Wildfire into the livery barn. Once outside again, he thrust a hand into his pocket and came up with his purse. He counted out a number of bills and gold coins and handed them to Sutton.

"There's the full two thousand dollars I owe you, Luke. I consider Wildfire to be worth twice that much, although I suppose I shouldn't tell you that or you might try to up your price on me."

Sutton smiled as he pocketed the money. "I want to wish you the best of luck in your breeding and racing programs back East. Wildfire'll be a credit to them both or I miss my guess."

"Oh, he will be, he will be."

"Well, I had best be moving on," Sutton said.

"Good-bye and good luck, Luke—and thank you again."

After they had shaken hands and Wilson had gone, Sutton went back inside the livery barn where he stood beside Wildfire's stall, watching the stallion eat the mix of oats and barley that the liveryman had placed in his feed bin.

He reached over the top of the stall and gently stroked the horse's neck and withers. "I'm glad I had a hand in seeing to it that no stud killer or anybody else for that matter got a chance to do you in, old fellow. You'll do fine back East in New Jersey. Mr. Wilson'll see to that. You'll have lots of ladies back there too, like I promised you, you old reprobate."

He turned and started out of the livery barn. At the door, he couldn't resist the strong impulse to turn and look once more and for the last time at Wildfire. As he did so, the horse raised its head and their eyes met. Sutton smartly touched the brim of his hat to the stallion. Wildfire nickered softly.

Sutton left the livery barn and headed up C Street, his destination the International Hotel. Along the way, as his thoughts of Wildfire began to give way to thoughts of the lovely Judith Fletcher, he stopped at a drugstore where, still thinking of Judith, he bought a bottle of bay rum.

"The ladies are most partial to the scent of bay rum," the clerk behind the counter commented as he bagged the purchase.

"I'm hoping one lady in particular likes it," Sutton said as he paid the clerk.

Got to shine my high-topped townsman's shoes, he thought, as he left the drugstore and resumed his journey. Got to buy myself a new shirt. Maybe a new hat

too. Might as well look the dandy for Miss Judith
Fletcher when she steps off the stage tomorrow.

He knew he would be there to meet her when she
did. With my hat thrown back and my spurs a-jin-
gling I will be, he promised himself, his pace quicken-
ing and a smile spreading across his face.

ABOUT THE AUTHOR

Leo P. Kelley has read and traveled widely, and his writing reflects his wide-ranging experience. He is the author of numerous Westerns, most notably the Luke Sutton series, which has seen the venerable Luke Sutton as an outlaw, a gunfighter, an Indian fighter, hired gun, bounty hunter, and lawman. *Luke Sutton: Mustanger* is the ninth book in the Luke Sutton series. His other Double D Westerns include *A Man Named Dundee* (1988) and *Morgan* (1987).

Mr. Kelley resides in Long Beach, New York.